Winnie-the-Pooh

クマのプーさん
WINNIE-THE-POOH
A.A.ミルン
A.A.MILNE

装幀 ● 菊地信義

装画 ● E. H. シェパード

ルビ ● 滝口峯子

Published by Kodansha International Ltd.,
17-14 Otowa 1-chome, Bunkyo-ku, Tokyo 112-8652.
No part of this publication may be reproduced
in any form or by any means without permission
in writing from the publisher.

WINNIE-THE-POOH
Text by A. A. Milne and line illustrations by E. H. Shepard.
Copyright under the Berne Convention.
Copyright © 1926 by E. P. Dutton. Copyright renewed 1954 by
A. A. Milne, with black and white line drawings by E. H. Shepard.
English language reprint in a paperback edition with Japanese
annotations rights arranged with The Trustees of the Pooh Properties
in care of Curtis Brown Group Ltd., London, through Tuttle-Mori
Agency, Inc., Tokyo

Copyright © 2001 by Kodansha International Ltd.
All rights reserved. Printed in Japan.
ISBN 4-7700-2474-6

本書について

　主人公はご存じのように、森に住む、ゆかいで楽しい動物の仲間たちと、クリストファー・ロビン少年です。著者のA. A. ミルン（Alan Alexander Milne）(1882-1956) が、幼い息子のロビン君のために作った、この童話のなかで、ロビン君が大好きだった動物のぬいぐるみたちは生命を吹き込まれ、わくわくどきどきする冒険を繰り広げていきます。
　続編の『プー横丁にたった家』と合わせて、20世紀を代表する不朽の児童文学として、世界中で愛されている作品です。

　　　　　　　　　　　＊　　＊
「トララー、トララー、トララー……」
　クマのプーさんが、楽しそうに鼻歌を歌いながら、森のなかを歩いています。突然、目の前に、砂の土手が現れました。そこに、大きな穴があいているのを見て、話し相手のほしかったプーさんは、頭を穴につっこんで、さけびました。
「だれか、いるの？」
　急にばたばたする音が聞こえたかと思うと、すぐに静かになりました。プーさんは、もう一度、大声をはりあげました。すると、
「いないよ！」「でっかい声でどならないで」
という言葉が返ってきました。プーさんは、穴から頭をだして、しばらく考え込んでから、また頭をつっこんで、たずねました。
「こんにちは、ウサギくんじゃないのかい？」
「ちがうよ！」
　ウサギは、今度は口調を変えて、返事をしました。

　　　　　　　　　　　＊　　＊
　A. A. ミルンは、ロンドンに生まれました。ケンブリッジ大学を卒業し、有名な風刺漫画週刊誌『パンチ』の副編集長となり、軽妙な随筆を同誌に載せました。第一次大戦後、文筆生活に入り、戯曲『ピム氏のお通り』や、推理小説の名作として知られる『赤い館の秘密』などを発表しました。3歳になったロビン君を寝かしつけるために作った童謡をまとめた『ぼくたちが小さかったとき』、および『ぼくたちは6歳』の2冊の本も高く評価されています。
　E. H. シェパード（Ernest H. Shepard）(1879-1976) はイギリスの風景画家、挿絵画家です。本書をはじめとするミルンの作品の挿絵で、不朽の名声を博しています。

To Her

Hand in hand we come
_{手に手を取って}
  Christopher Robin and I
  _{クリストファー・ロビン}
To lay this book in your lap.
                     _{ひざ}
  Say you're surprised?
  Say you like it?
  Say it's just what you wanted?
    Because it's yours—
    Because we love you.

INTRODUCTION
まえがき

If you happen to have read another book about Christopher Robin, you may remember that he once had a swan (or the swan had Christopher Robin, I don't know which) and that he used to call this swan Pooh. That was a long time ago, and when we said good-bye, we took the name with us, as we didn't think the swan would want it any more. Well, when Edward Bear said that he would like an exciting name all to himself, Christopher Robin said at once, without stopping to think, that he was Winnie-the-Pooh. And he was. So, as I have explained the Pooh part, I will now explain the rest of it.

You can't be in London for long without going to the Zoo. There are some people who begin the Zoo at the beginning, called WAYIN, and walk as quickly as they can past every cage until they get to the one called WAYOUT, but the nicest people go straight to the animal they love the most, and stay there. So when Christopher Robin goes to the Zoo, he goes to where the Polar Bears are, and he whispers something to the third keeper from the left, and doors are unlocked, and we wander through dark passages and up steep stairs, until at last we come to the special cage, and the cage is opened, and out trots something brown and furry, and with a happy cry of "Oh, Bear!" Christopher Robin rushes into its arms. Now this bear's name is Winnie, which shows what a good name for bears it is, but the funny thing is that we can't remember whether Winnie is called after Pooh, or Pooh after Winnie. We did know once, but we have forgotten....

I had written as far as this when Piglet looked up and said in his squeaky voice, "What about Me?" "My dear Piglet," I said, "the whole book is about you." "So it is about Pooh," he squeaked. You see what it is. He is jealous because he thinks Pooh is having a Grand Introduction all to himself. Pooh is the favourite, of course, there's no denying it, but Piglet comes in for a good many things which Pooh misses; because you can't take Pooh to school without everybody knowing it, but Piglet is so small that he slips into a pocket, where it is very comfortable to feel him when you are not quite sure whether twice seven is twelve or twenty-two. Sometimes he slips out and has a good look in the ink-pot, and in this way he has got more education than Pooh, but Pooh doesn't mind. Some have brains, and some haven't, he says, and there it is.

And not all the others are saying, "What about Us?" So perhaps the best thing to do is to stop writing Introductions and get on with the book.

A.A.M.

CONTENTS

Chapter I
In Which We Are Introduced to
Winnie-the-Pooh and Some Bees,
_{ウィニー・ザ・プー} _{みつばち}
and the Stories Begin ···17

Chapter II
In Which Pooh Goes Visiting
and Gets into a Tight Place ··36
_{きゅうくつな}

Chapter III
In Which Pooh and Piglet Go Hunting
_{ピグレット (コブタ)}
and Nearly Catch a Woozle 48
_{もう少しで} _{ウーズゥール}

Chapter IV
In Which Eeyore Loses a Tail
_{イーヨー} _{しっぽ}
and Pooh Finds One 58

Chapter V
In Which Piglet Meets a Heffalump 70
_{ヘファランプ}

CHAPTER VI

   In Which Eeyore Has a Birthday
   誕生日
   and Gets Two Presents ··86

CHAPTER VII

   In Which Kanga and Baby Roo Come to
   カンガ　　　　　ルー
   the Forest, and Piglet Has a Bath ··················104
   　　　　　　　　　　　　　　おふろに入る

CHAPTER VIII

   In Which Christopher Robin Leads
   an Expotition to the North Pole ····················124
   　=Expedition 探検　　　　　　北極

CHAPTER IX

   In Which Piglet Is Entirely Surrounded
   　　　　　　　　　完全に
   by Water ···144

CHAPTER X

   In Which Christopher Robin Gives
   Pooh a Party, and We Say Good-Bye ············161
   　　　パーティを開く

CHAPTER I

In Which
We Are Introduced to
Winnie-the-Pooh and Some Bees,
ウィニー・ザ・プー　　　　　　　みつばち
and the Stories Begin

Here is Edward Bear, coming downstairs, bump, bump, bump, on the back of his
ゴツン
head, behind Christopher Robin. It is, as far as he
彼の知るかぎりでは
knows, the only way of coming downstairs, but sometimes he feels that there really is another way,
やり方
if only he could stop bumping for a moment and
せめて~さえするならば
think of it. And then he feels that perhaps there isn't. Anyhow, here he is at the bottom, and ready to be introduced to you. Winnie-the-Pooh.

When I first heard his name, I said, just as you are going to say, "But I thought he was a boy?"

"So did I," said Christopher Robin.

"Then you can't call him Winnie?"
ウィニー

"I don't."

"But you said—"

"He's Winnie-ther-Pooh. Don't you know what
ウィニー・ザ・プー
'ther' means?"

"Ah, yes, now I do," I said quickly; and I hope you do too, because it is all the explanation you are going to get.

Sometimes Winnie-the-Pooh likes a game of some sort when he comes downstairs, and sometimes he likes to sit quietly in front of the fire and listen to a story. This evening—

"What about a story?" said Christopher Robin.

"*What* about a story?" I said.

"Could you very sweetly tell Winnie-the-Pooh one?"

"I suppose I could," I said. "What sort of stories does he like?"

"About himself. Because he's *that* sort of Bear."

"Oh, I see."

"So could you very sweetly?"

"I'll try," I said.

So I tried.

Once upon a time, a very long time ago now, about last Friday, Winnie-the-Pooh lived in a forest all by himself under the name of Sanders.

("What does 'under the name' mean?" asked Christopher Robin.

"It means he had the name over the door in gold letters, and lived under it."

"Winnie-the-Pooh wasn't quite sure," said Christopher Robin.

"Now I am," said a growly voice.
"Then I will go on," said I.)

One day when he was out walking, he came to an open place in the middle of the forest, and in the middle of this place was a large oak-tree, and, from the top of the tree, there came a loud buzzing-noise.

Winnie-the-Pooh sat down at the foot of the tree, put his head between his paws and began to think.

First of all he said to himself: "That buzzing-noise means something. You don't get a buzzing-noise like that, just buzzing and buzzing, without its meaning something. If there's a buzzing-noise, somebody's making a buzzing-noise, and the only reason for making a buzzing-noise that *I* know of is because you're a bee."

Then he thought another long time, and said: "And the only reason for being a bee that I know of is making honey."

And then he got up, and said: "And the only reason for making honey is so as *I* can eat it." So he began to climb the tree.

He
climbed
and
he
climbed
and
he
climbed,
and
as
he
climbed
he
sang
a
little
song
to
himself.
It
went
like
this:

Isn't it funny
How a bear likes honey?
Buzz! Buzz! Buzz!
ブンブン
I wonder why he does?

Then he climbed a little further…and a little further…and then just a little further. By that time he had thought of another song.

It's a very funny thought that, if Bears were Bees,
おかしな
They'd build their nests at the *bottom* of trees.
And that being so (if the Bees were Bears),
We shouldn't have to climb up all these stairs.

He was getting rather tired by this time, so that is why he sang a Complaining Song. He was near-
文句を言う
ly there now, and if he just stood on that branch…
乗っかりさえすれば　　　　枝
Crack!
バキッ

"Oh, help!" said Pooh, as he dropped ten feet to the branch below him.

"If only I hadn't—" he said, as he bounced twenty feet on to the next branch.

"You see, what I *meant* to do," he explained, as he turned head-over-heels, and crashed on to another branch thirty feet below, "what I *meant* to do—"

"Of course, it *was* rather—" he admitted, as he slithered very quickly through the next six branches.

"It all comes, I suppose," he decided, as he said good-bye to the last branch, spun round three times, and flew gracefully into a gorse-bush, "it all comes of *liking* honey so much. Oh, help!"

He crawled out of the gorse-bush, brushed the prickles from his nose, and began to think again. And the first person he thought of was Christopher Robin.

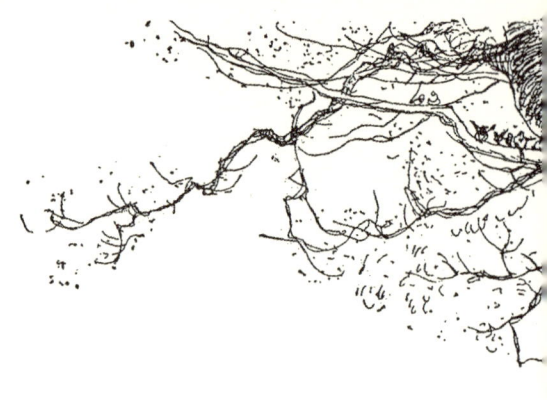

(*"Was that me?"* said Christopher Robin in an awed
voice, hardly daring to believe it.
　おどろいた
信じられないというように

"That was you."

Christopher Robin said nothing, but his eyes got
larger and larger, and his face got pinker and pinker.)
　　　　　　　　　　　　　　　　　　桃色になる

So Winnie-the-Pooh went round to his friend Christopher Robin, who lived behind a green door in another part of the Forest.

"Good morning, Christopher Robin," he said.

"Good morning, Winnie-*ther*-Pooh," said you.

"I wonder if you've got such a thing as a balloon about you?"

"A balloon?"

"Yes, I just said to myself coming along: 'I wonder if Christopher Robin has such a thing as a balloon about him?' I just said it to myself, thinking of balloons, and wondering."

"What do you want a balloon for?" you said.

Winnie-the-Pooh looked round to see that nobody was listening, put his paw to his mouth, and said in a deep whisper: *"Honey!"*

"But you don't get honey with balloons!"

"*I* do," said Pooh.

Well, it just happened that you had been to a party the day before at the house of your friend Piglet, and you had balloons at the party. You had had a big green balloon; and one of Rabbit's relations had had a big blue one, and had left it behind, being really too young to go to a party at all; and so you had brought the green one *and* the blue one home with you.

"Which one would you like?" you asked Pooh.

He put his head between his paws and thought very carefully.

"It's like this," he said. "When you go after honey with a balloon, the great thing is not to let the bees know you're coming. Now, if you have a green balloon, they might think you were only part of the tree, and not notice you, and if you have a blue balloon, they might think you were only part of the sky, and not notice you, and the question is: Which is most likely?"

"Wouldn't they notice *you* underneath the balloon?" you asked.

"They might or they might not," said Winnie-the-Pooh. "You never can tell with bees." He thought for a moment and said: "I shall try to look like a small black cloud. That will deceive them."

"Then you had better have the blue balloon," you said; and so it was decided.

Well, you both went out with the blue balloon, and you took your gun with you, just in case, as you always did, and Winnie-the-Pooh went to a very muddy place that he knew of, and rolled and rolled until he was black all over; and then, when the balloon was blown up as big as big,

and you and Pooh were both holding on to the string, you let go suddenly, and Pooh Bear floated gracefully up into the sky, and stayed there—level with the top of the tree and about twenty feet away from it.

"Hooray!" you shouted.

"Isn't that fine?" shouted Winnie-the-Pooh down to you. "What do I look like?"

"You look like a Bear holding on to a balloon," you said.

"Not," said Pooh anxiously, "—not like a small black cloud in a blue sky?"

"Not very much."

"Ah, well, perhaps from up here it looks different. And, as I say, you never can tell with bees."

There was no wind to blow him nearer to the tree, so there he stayed. He could see the honey,

he could smell the honey, but he couldn't quite reach the honey.
 とどく

After a little while he called down to you.

"Christopher Robin!" he said in a loud whisper.

"Hallo!"

"I think the bees suspect something!"
 うたがう

"What sort of thing?"

"I don't know. But something tells me that they're suspicious!"
 うたがっている

"Perhaps they think that you're after their honey."
 狙って

"It may be that. You never can tell with bees."

There was another little silence, and then he called down to you again.

"Christopher Robin!"

"Yes?"

"Have you an umbrella in your house?"

"I think so."

"I wish you would bring it out here, and walk up and down with it, and look up at me every
 ときどき

now and then, and say 'Tut-tut, it looks like rain.'
I think, if you did that, it would help the deception which we are practising on these bees."

Well, you laughed to yourself, "Silly old Bear!" but you didn't say it aloud because you were so fond of him, and you went home for your umbrella.

"Oh, there you are!" called down Winnie-the-Pooh, as soon as you got back to the tree. "I was beginning to get anxious. I have discovered that the bees are definitely Suspicious."

"Shall I put my umbrella up?" you said.

"Yes, but wait a moment. We must be practical. The important bee to deceive is the Queen Bee. Can you see which is the Queen Bee from down there?"

"No."

"A pity. Well, now, if you walk up and down with your umbrella, saying, 'Tut-tut, it looks like rain,' I shall do what I can by singing a little Cloud Song, such as a cloud might sing.... Go!"

So, while you walked up and down and wondered if it would rain, Winnie-the-Pooh sang this song:

> How sweet to be a Cloud
> Floating in the Blue!
> 浮かんで
> Every little cloud
> *Always* sings aloud.

"How sweet to be a Cloud
    Floating in the Blue!"
It makes him very proud
            誇らしく
To be a little cloud.

The bees were still buzzing as suspiciously as
                    ブンブンいう
ever. Some of them, indeed, left their nest and
                    なんと
flew all round the cloud as it began the second

verse of this song, and one bee sat down on the nose of the cloud for a moment, and then got up again.

"Christopher—*ow!*—Robin," called out the cloud.

"Yes?"

"I have just been thinking, and I have come to a very important decision. *These are the wrong sort of bees.*"

"Are they?"

"Quite the wrong sort. So I should think they would make the wrong sort of honey, shouldn't you?"

"Would they?"

"Yes. So I think I shall come down."

"How?" asked you.

Winnie-the-Pooh hadn't thought about this. If he let go of the string, he would fall—*bump*—and he didn't like the idea of that. So he thought for a long time, and then he said:

"Christopher Robin, you must shoot the balloon with your gun. Have you got your gun?"

"Of course I have," you said. "But if I do that, it will spoil the balloon," you said.

"But if you *don't*," said Pooh, "I shall have to let go, and that would spoil *me*."

When he put it like this, you saw how it was, and you aimed very carefully at the balloon, and fired.
_{狙う}

"*Ow!*" said Pooh.

"Did I miss?" you asked.
_{はずす}

"You didn't exactly *miss*," said Pooh, "but you missed the *balloon*."

"I'm so sorry," you said, and you fired again, and this time you hit the balloon, and the air
_{こんど}
came slowly out, and Winnie-the-Pooh floated down to the ground.

But his arms were so stiff from holding on to the string of the balloon all that time that they stayed up straight in the air for more than a week, and whenever a fly came and settled on his nose he had to blow it off. And I think—but I am not sure—that *that* is why he was always called Pooh.

"Is that the end of the story?" asked Christopher Robin.

"That's the end of that one. There are others."

"About Pooh and Me?"

"And Piglet and Rabbit and all of you. Don't you remember?"

"I do remember, and then when I try to remember, I forget."

"That day when Pooh and Piglet tried to catch the Heffalump—"

"They didn't catch it, did they?"

"No."

"Pooh couldn't, because he hasn't any brain. Did *I* catch it?"

"Well, that comes into the story."

Christopher Robin nodded.

"I do remember," he said, "only Pooh doesn't very well, so that's why he likes having it told to him again. Because then it's a real story and not just a remembering."

"That's just how *I* feel."

Christopher Robin gave a deep sigh, picked his Bear up by the leg, and walked off to the door, trailing Pooh behind him. At the door he turned and said, "Coming to see me have my bath?"

"I might," I said.

"I didn't hurt him when I shot him, did I?"

"Not a bit."

He nodded and went out, and in a moment I heard Winnie-the-Pooh—*bump, bump, bump*—going up the stairs behind him.

CHAPTER II

In Which
Pooh Goes Visiting
and Gets into a Tight Place
きゅつな

Edward Bear, known to his friends as Winnie-the-Pooh, or Pooh for short, was walking
略して
through the forest one day, humming proudly to
鼻歌を歌って 得意そうに
himself. He had made up a little hum that very
morning, as he was doing his Stoutness Exercises
じょうぶになるための 体操
in front of the glass: *Tra-la-la, tra-la-la,* as he
トラララー
stretched up as high as he could go, and then *Tra-*
体をのばす
la-la, tra-la—oh, help!—la, as he tried to reach his
toes. After breakfast he had said it over and over
足のつまさき
to himself until he had learnt it off by heart, and
暗記して

now he was humming it right through, properly. It went like this:

> *Tra-la-la, tra-la-la,*
> *Tra-la-la, tra-la-la,*
> *Rum-tum-tiddle-um-tum.*
> *Tiddle-iddle, tiddle-iddle,*
> *Tiddle-iddle, tiddle-iddle,*
> *Rum-tum-tum-tiddle-um.*

Well, he was humming this hum to himself, and walking along gaily, wondering what everybody else was doing, and what it felt like being somebody else, when suddenly he came to a sandy bank, and in the bank was a large hole.

"Aha!" said Pooh. (*Rum-tum-tiddle-um-tum.*) "If I know anything about anything, that hole means Rabbit," he said, "and Rabbit means Company," he said, "and Company means Food and Listening-to-Me-Humming and such like. *Rum-tum-tum-tiddle-um.*"

So he bent down, put his head into the hole, and called out:

"Is anybody at home?"

There was a sudden scuffling noise from inside the hole, and then silence.

"What I said was, 'Is anybody at home?'" called out Pooh very loudly.

"No!" said a voice; and then added, "you needn't shout so loud. I heard you quite well the first time."

"Bother!" said Pooh. "Isn't there anybody here at all?"

"Nobody."

Winnie-the-Pooh took his head out of the hole, and thought for a little, and he thought to himself, "There must be somebody there, because somebody must have *said* 'Nobody.'" So he put his head back in the hole, and said:

"Hallo, Rabbit, isn't that you?"

"No," said Rabbit, in a different sort of voice this time.

"But isn't that Rabbit's voice?"

"I don't *think* so," said Rabbit. "It isn't *meant* to be."

"Oh!" said Pooh.

He took his head out of the hole, and had another think, and then he put it back, and said:

"Well, could you very kindly tell me where Rabbit is?"

"He has gone to see his friend Pooh Bear, who is a great friend of his."

"But this *is* Me!" said Bear, very much surprised.

"What sort of Me?"

"Pooh Bear."

"Are you sure?" said Rabbit, still more surprised.

"Quite, quite sure," said Pooh.

"Oh, well, then, come in."

So Pooh pushed and pushed and pushed his way through the hole, and at last he got in.

"You were quite right," said Rabbit, looking at him all over. "It *is* you. Glad to see you."

"Who did you think it was?"

"Well, I wasn't sure. You know how it is in the Forest. One can't have *anybody* coming into one's house. One has to be *careful*. What about a mouthful of something?"

Pooh always liked a little something at eleven o'clock in the morning, and he was very glad to see Rabbit getting out the plates and mugs; and when Rabbit said, "Honey or condensed milk with your bread?" he was so excited that he said, "Both," and then, so as not to seem greedy, he added, "but don't bother about the bread, please." And for a long time after that he said nothing...until at last, humming to himself in a rather sticky voice, he got up, shook Rabbit lovingly by the paw, and said that he must be going on.

"Must you?" said Rabbit politely.

"Well," said Pooh, "I could stay a little longer if it—if you—" and he tried very hard to look in the direction of the larder.

"As a matter of fact," said Rabbit, "I was going out myself directly."

"Oh, well, then, I'll be going on. Good-bye."

"Well, good-bye, if you're sure you won't have any more."

"*Is* there any more?" asked Pooh quickly.

Rabbit took the covers off the dishes, and said no, there wasn't.

"I thought not," said Pooh, nodding to himself. "Well, good-bye. I must be going on."

So he started to climb out of the hole. He pulled with his front paws, and pushed with his back paws, and in a little while his nose was out in the open again...and then his ears...and then his front paws...and then his shoulders...and then—

"Oh, help!" said Pooh. "I'd better go back."

"Oh, bother!" said Pooh. "I shall have to go on."

"I can't do either!" said Pooh. "Oh, help *and* bother!"

Now by this time Rabbit wanted to go for a walk too, and finding the front door full, he went out by the back door, and came round to Pooh, and looked at him.

"Hallo, are you stuck?" he asked.

"N-no," said Pooh carelessly. "Just resting and thinking and humming to myself."

"Here, give us a paw."

Pooh Bear stretched out a paw, and Rabbit pulled and pulled and pulled....

"*Ow!*" cried Pooh. "You're hurting!"

"The fact is," said Rabbit, "you're stuck."

"It all comes," said Pooh crossly, "of not having front doors big enough."

"It all comes," said Rabbit sternly, "of eating too much. I thought at the time," said Rabbit, "only I didn't like to say anything," said Rabbit, "that one of us was eating too much," said Rabbit, "and I knew it wasn't *me*," he said. "Well, well, I shall go and fetch Christopher Robin."

Christopher Robin lived at the other end of the Forest, and when he came back with Rabbit, and saw the front half of Pooh, he said, "Silly old Bear," in such a loving voice that everybody felt quite hopeful again.

"I was just beginning to think," said Bear, sniffing slightly, "that Rabbit might never be able to use his front door again. And I should *hate* that," he said.

"So should I," said Rabbit.

"Use his front door again?" said Christopher Robin. "Of course he'll use his front door again."

"Good," said Rabbit.

"If we can't pull you out, Pooh, we might push you back."

Rabbit scratched his whiskers thoughtfully, and pointed out that, when once Pooh was pushed back, he was back, and of course nobody was more glad to see Pooh than *he* was, still there it was, some lived in trees and some lived underground, and—

"You mean I'd *never* get out?" said Pooh.

"I mean," said Rabbit, "that having got *so* far, it seems a pity to waste it."

Christopher Robin nodded.

"Then there's only one thing to be done," he said. "We shall have to wait for you to get thin again."

"How long does getting thin take?" asked Pooh anxiously.

"About a week, I should think."

"But I can't stay here for a *week*!"

"You can *stay* here all right, silly old Bear. It's getting you out which is so difficult."

"We'll read to you," said Rabbit cheerfully. "And I hope it won't snow," he added. "And I say, old fellow, you're taking up a good deal of room in my house—*do* you mind if I use your back legs as a towel-horse? Because, I mean, there they are—doing nothing—and it would be very convenient just to hang the towels on them."

"A week!" said Pooh gloomily. "*What about meals?*"

"I'm afraid no meals," said Christopher Robin, "because of getting thin quicker. But we *will* read to you."

Bear began to sigh, and then found he couldn't because he was so tightly stuck; and a tear rolled down his eye, as he said:

"Then would you read a Sustaining Book, such

as would help and comfort a Wedged Bear in Great Tightness?"

So for a week Christopher Robin read that sort of book at the North end of Pooh, and Rabbit...

hung his washing on the South end...and in between

Bear felt himself getting slenderer and slenderer. And at the end of the week Christopher Robin said, *"Now!"*

So he took hold of Pooh's front paws and Rabbit took hold of Christopher Robin, and all Rabbit's friends and relations took hold of Rabbit, and they all pulled together....

And for a long time Pooh only said *"Ow!"*...
And *"Oh!"*...

And then, all of a sudden, he said *"Pop!"* just as if a cork were coming out of a bottle.

And Christopher Robin and Rabbit and all Rabbit's friends and relations went head-over-heels backwards...and on top of them came Winnie-the-Pooh—free!

So, with a nod of thanks to his friends, he went on with his walk through the forest, humming proudly to himself. But Christopher Robin looked after him lovingly, and said to himself, "Silly old Bear!"

CHAPTER III

In Which
Pooh and Piglet Go Hunting
and Nearly Catch a Woozle

The Piglet lived in a very grand house in the middle of a beech-tree, and the beech-tree was in the middle of the forest, and the Piglet lived in the middle of the house. Next to his house was a piece of broken board which had: "TRESPASSERS W" on it. When Christopher Robin asked the Piglet what it meant, he said it was his grandfather's name, and had been in the family for a long time. Christopher Robin said you *couldn't* be called Trespassers W, and Piglet said yes, you could, because his grandfather was, and it was short for Trespassers Will, which was short for Trespassers William. And his grandfather had had two names in case he lost one—Trespassers after an uncle, and William after Trespassers.

"I've got two names," said Christopher Robin carelessly.

"Well, there you are, that proves it," said Piglet.

One fine winter's day when Piglet was brushing away the snow in front of his house, he happened to look up, and there was Winnie-the-Pooh. Pooh was walking round and round in a circle, thinking of something else, and when Piglet called to him, he just went on walking.

"Hallo!" said Piglet, "what are *you* doing?"

"Hunting," said Pooh.

"Hunting what?"

"Tracking something," said Winnie-the-Pooh very mysteriously.

"Tracking what?" said Piglet, coming closer.

"That's just what I ask myself. I ask myself, What?"

"What do you think you'll answer?"

"I shall have to wait until I catch up with it," said Winnie-the-Pooh. "Now, look there." He pointed to the ground in front of him. "What do you see there?"

"Tracks," said Piglet. "Paw-marks." He gave a little squeak of excitement. "Oh, Pooh! Do you think it's a—a—a Woozle?"

"It may be," said Pooh. "Sometimes it is, and sometimes it isn't. You never can tell with paw-marks."

With these few words he went on tracking, and Piglet, after watching him for a minute or two, ran after him. Winnie-the-Pooh had come to a sudden stop, and was bending over the tracks in a puzzled sort of way.

"What's the matter?" asked Piglet.

"It's a very funny thing," said Bear, "but there seem to be *two* animals now. This—whatever-it-was—has been joined by another—whatever-it-is—and the two of them are now proceeding in company. Would you mind coming with me, Piglet, in case they turn out to be Hostile Animals?"

Piglet scratched his ear in a nice sort of way, and said that he had nothing to do until Friday, and would be delighted to come, in case it really *was* a Woozle.

"You mean, in case it really is two Woozles," said Winnie-the-Pooh, and Piglet said that anyhow he had nothing to do until Friday. So off they went together.

There was a small spinney of larch trees just here, and it seemed as if the two Woozles, if that is what they were, had been going round this spinney; so round this spinney went Pooh and Piglet after them; Piglet passing the time by telling Pooh what his Grandfather Trespassers W had done to Remove Stiffness after Tracking, and how his Grandfather Trespassers W had suffered in his later years from Shortness of Breath, and other matters of interest, and Pooh wondering what a Grandfather was like, and if perhaps this was Two Grandfathers they were after now, and, if so, whether he would be allowed to take one home and keep it, and what Christopher Robin would say. And still the tracks went on in front of them....

Suddenly Winnie-the-Pooh stopped and pointed excitedly in front of him. "*Look!*"

"What?" said Piglet, with a jump. And then, to show that he hadn't been frightened, he jumped up and down once or twice in an exercising sort of way.

"The tracks!" said Pooh. "*A third animal has joined the other two!*"

"Pooh!" cried Piglet. "Do you think it is another Woozle?"

"No," said Pooh, "because it makes different

marks. It is either Two Woozles and one, as it might be, Wizzle, or Two, as it might be, Wizzles and one, if so it is, Woozle. Let us continue to follow them."

So they went on, feeling just a little anxious now, in case the three animals in front of them were of Hostile Intent. And Piglet wished very much that his Grandfather T. W. were there, instead of elsewhere, and Pooh thought how nice it would be if they met Christopher Robin suddenly but quite accidentally, and only because he liked Christopher Robin so much. And then, all of a sudden, Winnie-the-Pooh stopped again, and licked the tip of his nose in a cooling manner, for he was feeling more hot and anxious than ever in his life before. *There were four animals in front of them!*

"Do you see, Piglet? Look at their tracks! Three, as it were, Woozles, and one, as it was, Wizzle. Another Woozle has joined them!"

And so it seemed to be. There were the tracks; crossing over each other here, getting muddled up with each other there; but, quite plainly every now and then, the tracks of four sets of paws.

"I think," said Piglet, when he had licked the tip of his nose too, and found that it brought very little comfort, "I think that I have just remembered something. I have just remembered something that I forgot to do yesterday and sha'n't be able to do tomorrow. So I suppose I really ought to go back and do it now."

"We'll do it this afternoon, and I'll come with you," said Pooh.

"It isn't the sort of thing you can do in the afternoon," said Piglet quickly. "It's a very particular morning thing, that has to be done in the morning, and, if possible, between the hours of— What would you say the time was?"

"About twelve," said Winnie-the-Pooh, looking at the sun.

"Between, as I was saying, the hours of twelve and twelve five. So, really, dear old Pooh, if you'll excuse me— What's that?"

Pooh looked up at the sky, and then, as he heard the whistle again, he looked up into the branches of a big oak-tree, and then he saw a friend of his.

"It's Christopher Robin," he said.

"Ah, then you'll be all right," said Piglet. "You'll be quite safe with *him*. Good-bye," and he trotted off home as quickly as he could, very glad to be Out of All Danger again.

Christopher Robin came slowly down his tree.

"Silly old Bear," he said, "what *were* you doing? First you went round the spinney twice by yourself, and then Piglet ran after you and you went round together, and then you were just going round a fourth time—"

"Wait a minute," said Winnie-the-Pooh, holding up his paw.

He sat down and thought, in the most thoughtful way he could think. Then he fitted his paw into one of the Tracks…and then he scratched his nose twice, and stood up.

"Yes," said Winnie-the-Pooh.

"I see now," said Winnie-the-Pooh.

"I have been Foolish and Deluded," he said, "and I am a Bear of No Brain at All."

"You're the Best Bear in All the World," said Christopher Robin soothingly.

"Am I?" said Pooh hopefully. And then he brightened up suddenly.

"Anyhow," he said, "it is nearly Luncheon Time."

So he went home for it.

CHAPTER IV

In Which
Eeyore Loses a Tail
and Pooh Finds One

The old grey donkey, Eeyore, stood by himself in a thistly corner of the forest, his front feet well apart, his head on one side, and thought about things. Sometimes he thought sadly to himself, "Why?" and sometimes he thought, "Wherefore?" and sometimes he thought, "Inasmuch as which?"—and sometimes he didn't quite know what he *was* thinking about. So when Winnie-the-Pooh came stumping along, Eeyore was very glad to be able to stop thinking for a little, in order to say "How do you do?" in a gloomy manner to him.

"And how are you?" said Winnie-the-Pooh.

Eeyore shook his head from side to side.

"Not very how," he said. "I don't seem to have felt at all how for a long time."

"Dear, dear," said Pooh, "I'm sorry about that. Let's have a look at you."

So Eeyore stood there, gazing sadly at the ground, and Winnie-the-Pooh walked all round him once.

"Why, what's happened to your tail?" he said in surprise.

"What *has* happened to it?" said Eeyore.
"It isn't there!"
"Are you sure?"

"Well, either a tail *is* there or it isn't there. You can't make a mistake about it. And yours *isn't* there!"

"Then what is?"

"Nothing."

"Let's have a look," said Eeyore, and he turned slowly round to the place where his tail had been a little while ago, and then, finding that he couldn't catch it up, he turned round the other way, until he came back to where he was at first, and then he put his head down and looked between his front legs, and at last he said, with a long, sad sigh, "I believe you're right."

"Of course I'm right," said Pooh.

"That Accounts for a Good Deal," said Eeyore gloomily. "It Explains Everything. No Wonder."

"You must have left it somewhere," said Winnie-the-Pooh.

"Somebody must have taken it," said Eeyore. "How Like Them," he added, after a long silence.

Pooh felt that he ought to say something helpful about it, but didn't quite know what. So he decided to do something helpful instead.

"Eeyore," he said solemnly, "I, Winnie-the-Pooh, will find your tail for you."

"Thank you, Pooh," answered Eeyore. "You're a real friend," said he. "Not Like Some," he said.

So Winnie-the-Pooh went off to find Eeyore's tail.

It was a fine spring morning in the Forest as he started out. Little soft clouds played happily in a blue sky, skipping from time to time in front of the sun as if they had come to put it out, and then sliding away suddenly so that the next might have his turn. Through them and between them the sun shone bravely; and a copse which had worn its firs all the year round seemed old and dowdy now beside the new green lace which the beeches had put on so prettily. Through copse and spinney marched Bear; down open slopes of gorse and heather, over rocky beds of streams, up steep banks of sandstone into the heather again; and so at last, tired and hungry, to the Hundred Acre Wood. For it was in the Hundred Acre Wood that Owl lived.

"And if anyone knows anything about anything," said Bear to himself, "it's Owl who knows something about something," he said, "or my name's not Winnie-the-Pooh," he said. "Which it is," he added. "So there you are."

Owl lived at The Chestnuts, an old-world residence of great charm, which was grander than anybody else's, or seemed so to Bear, because it had both a knocker *and* a bell-pull. Underneath the knocker there was a notice which said:

PLES RING IF AN RNSER IS REQIRD.
= PLEASE   = ANSWER   =REQUIRED

Underneath the bell-pull there was a notice which said:

PLEZ CNOKE IF AN RNSR IS NOT REQID.
= KNOCK   =ANSWER   = REQUIRED

These notices had been written by Christopher

PLES RING IF AN RNSR IS REQIRD
PLEZ CNOKE IF AN RNSR IS NOT REQID

Robin, who was the only one in the forest who could spell; for Owl, wise though he was in many ways, able to read and write and spell his own name WOL, yet somehow went all to pieces over delicate words like MEASLES and BUTTERED TOAST.

Winnie-the-Pooh read the two notices very carefully, first from left to right, and afterwards, in case he had missed some of it, from right to left. Then, to make quite sure, he knocked and pulled the knocker, and he pulled and knocked the bell-rope, and he called out in a very loud voice, "Owl! I require an answer! It's Bear speaking." And the door opened, and Owl looked out.

"Hallo, Pooh," he said. "How's things?"

"Terrible and Sad," said Pooh, "because Eeyore, who is a friend of mine, has lost his tail. And he's Moping about it. So could you very kindly tell me how to find it for him?"

"Well," said Owl, "the customary procedure in such cases is as follows."

"What does Crustimoney Proseedcake mean?" said Pooh. "For I am a Bear of Very Little Brain, and long words Bother me."

"It means the Thing to Do."

"As long as it means that, I don't mind," said Pooh humbly.

"The thing to do is as follows. First, Issue a Reward. Then—"

"Just a moment," said Pooh, holding up his paw. "*What* do we do to this—what you were saying? You sneezed just as you were going to tell me."

"I *didn't* sneeze."

"Yes, you did, Owl."

"Excuse me, Pooh, I didn't. You can't sneeze without knowing it."

"Well, you can't know it without something having been sneezed."

"What I *said* was, 'First *Issue* a Reward.'"

"You're doing it again," said Pooh sadly.

"A Reward!" said Owl very loudly. "We write a notice to say that we will give a large something to anybody who finds Eeyore's tail."

"I see, I see," said Pooh, nodding his head. "Talking about large somethings," he went on dreamily, "I generally have a small something about now—about this time in the morning," and he looked wistfully at the cupboard in the corner of Owl's parlour; "just a mouthful of condensed milk or what-not, with perhaps a lick of honey—"

"Well, then," said Owl, "we write out this notice, and we put it up all over the Forest."

"A lick of honey," murmured Bear to himself, "or—or not, as the case may be." And he gave a deep sigh, and tried very hard to listen to what Owl was saying.

But Owl went on and on, using longer and longer words, until at last he came back to where he started, and he explained that the person to write out this notice was Christopher Robin.

"It was he who wrote the ones on my front door for me. Did you see them, Pooh?"

For some time now Pooh had been saying "Yes" and "No" in turn, with his eyes shut, to all that Owl was saying, and having said, "Yes, yes," last time, he said, "No, not at all," now, without really knowing what Owl was talking about.

"Didn't you see them?" said Owl, a little surprised. "Come and look at them now."

So they went outside. And Pooh looked at the knocker and the notice below it, and he looked at the bell-rope and the notice below it, and the more he looked at the bell-rope, the more he felt that he had seen something like it, somewhere else, sometime before.

"Handsome bell-rope, isn't it?" said Owl.

Pooh nodded.

"It reminds me of something," he said, "but I can't think what. Where did you get it?"

"I just came across it in the Forest. It was hanging over a bush, and I thought at first somebody lived there, so I rang it, and nothing happened, and then I rang it again very loudly, and it came off in my hand, and as nobody seemed to want it, I took it home, and—"

"Owl," said Pooh solemnly, "you made a mistake. Somebody did want it."

"Who?"

"Eeyore. My dear friend Eeyore. He was—he was fond of it."

"Fond of it?"

"Attached to it," said Winnie-the-Pooh sadly.

So with these words he unhooked it, and carried it back to Eeyore; and when Christopher Robin had nailed it on in its right place again, Eeyore frisked about the forest, waving his tail so happily that Winnie-the-Pooh came over all funny, and had to hurry home for a little snack of something to sustain him. And, wiping his mouth half an hour afterwards, he sang to himself proudly:

Who found the Tail?
"I," said Pooh,
At a quarter to two
(Only it was quarter to eleven really),
I found the Tail!"

CHAPTER V

In Which
Piglet Meets a Heffalump

One day, when Christopher Robin and Winnie-the-Pooh and Piglet were all talking together, Christopher Robin finished the mouthful he was eating and said carelessly: "I saw a Heffalump to-day, Piglet."

"What was it doing?," asked Piglet.

"Just lumping along," said Christopher Robin. "I don't think it saw *me*."

"I saw one once," said Piglet. "At least, I think I did," he said. "Only perhaps it wasn't."

"So did I," said Pooh, wondering what a Heffalump was like.

"You don't often see them," said Christopher Robin carelessly.

"Not now," said Piglet.

"Not at this time of year," said Pooh.

Then they all talked about something else, until

it was time for Pooh and Piglet to go home together. At first as they stumped along the path which edged the Hundred Acre Wood, they didn't say much to each other; but when they came to the stream and had helped each other across the stepping stones, and were able to walk side by side again over the heather, they began to talk in a friendly way about this and that, and Piglet said, "If you see what I mean, Pooh," and Pooh said, "It's just what I think myself, Piglet," and Piglet said, "But, on the other hand, Pooh, we must remember," and Pooh said, "Quite true, Piglet, although I had forgotten it for the moment." And then, just as they came to the Six Pine Trees, Pooh looked round to see that nobody else was listening, and said in a very solemn voice:

"Piglet, I have decided something."

"What have you decided, Pooh?"

"I have decided to catch a Heffalump."

Pooh nodded his head several times as he said this, and waited for Piglet to say "How?" or "Pooh, you couldn't!" or something helpful of that sort, but Piglet said nothing. The fact was Piglet was wishing that *he* had thought about it first.

"I shall do it," said Pooh, after waiting a little longer, "by means of a trap. And it must be a Cunning Trap, so you will have to help me, Piglet."

"Pooh," said Piglet, feeling quite happy again now, "I will." And then he said, "How shall we do it?" and Pooh said, "That's just it. How?" And then they sat down together to think it out.

Pooh's first idea was that they should dig a Very Deep Pit, and then the Heffalump would come along and fall into the Pit, and—

"Why?" said Piglet.

"Why what?" said Pooh.

"Why would he fall in?"

Pooh rubbed his nose with his paw, and said that the Heffalump might be walking along, humming a little song, and looking up at the sky, wondering if it would rain, and so he wouldn't see the Very Deep Pit until he was half-way down, when it would be too late.

Piglet said that this was a very good Trap, but supposing it were raining already?

Pooh rubbed his nose again, and said that he hadn't thought of that. And then he brightened up, and said that, if it were raining already, the Heffalump would be looking at the sky wondering it if would *clear up*, and so he wouldn't see the Very Deep Pit until he was half-way down.... When it would be too late.

Piglet said that, now that this point had been explained, he thought it was a Cunning Trap.

Pooh was very proud when he heard this, and he felt that the Heffalump was as good as caught already, but there was just one other thing which had to be thought about, and it was this. *Where should they dig the Very Deep Pit?*

Piglet said that the best place would be somewhere where a Heffalump was, just before he fell into it, only about a foot farther on.

"But then he would see us digging it," said Pooh.

"Not if he was looking at the sky."

"He would Suspect," said Pooh, "if he happened to look down." He thought for a long time and then added sadly, "It isn't as easy as I thought. I suppose that's why Heffalumps hardly *ever* get caught."

"That must be it," said Piglet.

They sighed and got up; and when they had taken a few gorse prickles out of themselves they sat down again; and all the time Pooh was saying to himself, "If only I could *think* of something!" For he felt sure that a Very Clever Brain could catch a Heffalump if only he knew the right way to go about it.

"Suppose," he said to Piglet, "*you* wanted to catch *me*, how would you do it?"

"Well," said Piglet, "I should do it like this. I should make a Trap, and I should put a Jar of Honey in the Trap, and you would smell it, and you would go in after it, and—"

"And I would go in after it," said Pooh excitedly, "only very carefully so as not to hurt myself, and I would get to the Jar of Honey, and I should lick round the edges first of all, pretending that there wasn't any more, you know, and then I should walk away and think about it a little, and then I should come back and start licking in the middle of the jar, and then—"

"Yes, well never mind about that. There you would be, and there I should catch you. Now the first thing to think of is, What do Heffalumps like? I should think acorns, shouldn't you? We'll get a lot of—I say, wake up, Pooh!"

Pooh, who had gone into a happy dream, woke up with a start, and said that Honey was a much more trappy thing than Haycorns. Piglet didn't think so; and they were just going to argue

74

about it, when Piglet remembered that, if they put acorns in the Trap, *he* would have to find the acorns, but if they put honey, then Pooh would have to give up some of his own honey, so he said, "All right, honey then," just as Pooh remembered it too, and was going to say, "All right, haycorns."

"Honey," said Piglet to himself in a thoughtful way, as if it were now settled. "*I'll* dig the pit, while *you* go and get the honey."

"Very well," said Pooh, and he stumped off.

As soon as he got home, he went to the larder; and he stood on a chair, and took down a very large jar of honey from the top shelf. It had HUNNY written on it, but, just to make sure, he took off the paper cover and looked at it, and it *looked* just like honey. "But you never can tell," said Pooh. "I remember my uncle saying once that he had seen cheese just this colour." So he put his tongue in, and took a large lick. "Yes," he said, "it is. No doubt about that. And honey, I should say, right down to the bottom of the jar. Unless, of course," he said, "somebody put cheese in at the bottom just for a joke. Perhaps I had better go a *little* further...just in case...in case Heffalumps *don't* like cheese...same as me.... Ah!" And he gave a deep sigh. "I *was* right. It *is* honey, right the way down."

Having made certain of this, he took the jar back to Piglet, and Piglet looked up from the bottom of his Very Deep Pit, and said "Got it?" and

Pooh said, "Yes, but it isn't quite a full jar," and he threw it down to Piglet, and Piglet said, "No, it isn't! Is that all you've got left?" and Pooh said "Yes." Because it was. So Piglet put the jar at the bottom of the Pit, and climbed out, and they went off home together.

"Well, good night, Pooh," said Piglet, when they had got to Pooh's house. "And we meet at six o'clock tomorrow morning by the Pine Trees, and see how many Heffalumps we've got in our Trap."

"Six o'clock, Piglet. And have you got any string?"

"No. Why do you want string?"

"To lead them home with."

"Oh!...I *think* Heffalumps come if you whistle."

"Some do and some don't. You never can tell with Heffalumps. Well, good night!"

"Good night!"

And off Piglet trotted to his house, Trespassers W, while Pooh made his preparations for bed.

Some hours later, just as the night was beginning to steal away, Pooh woke up suddenly with a sinking feeling. He had had that sinking feeling before, and he knew what it meant. *He was hungry.* So he went to the larder, and he stood on a chair and reached up to the top shelf, and found—nothing.

"That's funny," he thought. "I know I had a jar of honey there. A full jar, full of honey right up to the top, and it had HUNNY written on it, so that I should know it was honey. That's very funny." And then he began to wander up and down, wondering where it was and murmuring a murmur to himself. Like this:

> It's very, very funny,
> 'Cos I *know* I had some honey;
> 'Cos it had a label on,
>   Saying HUNNY.
>
> A goloptious full-up pot too,
> And I don't know where it's got to,
> No, I don't know where it's gone—
>   Well, it's funny.

He had murmured this to himself three times in a singing sort of way, when suddenly he remembered. He had put it into the Cunning Trap to catch the Heffalump.

"Bother!" said Pooh. "It all comes of trying to be kind to Heffalumps." And he got back into bed.

But he couldn't sleep. The more he tried to sleep, the more he couldn't. He tried Counting Sheep, which is sometimes a good way of getting to sleep, and, as that was no good, he tried counting Heffalumps. And that was worse. Because every Heffalump that he counted was making straight for a pot of Pooh's honey, and *eating it all*. For some minutes he lay there miserably, but when the five hundred and eighty-seventh Heffalump was licking its jaws, and saying to itself, "Very good honey this, I don't know when I've tasted better," Pooh could bear it no longer. He jumped out of bed, he ran out of the house, and he ran straight to the Six Pine Trees.

The Sun was still in bed, but there was a lightness in the sky over the Hundred Acre Wood which seemed to show that it was waking up and would soon be kicking off the clothes. In the half-light the Pine Trees looked cold and lonely, and the Very Deep Pit seemed deeper than it was, and Pooh's jar of honey at the bottom was something mysterious, a shape and no more. But as he got nearer to it his nose told him that it was indeed honey, and his tongue came out and began to polish up his mouth, ready for it.

"Bother!" said Pooh, as he got his nose inside the jar. "A Heffalump has been eating it!" And then he thought a little and said, "Oh, no, *I* did. I forgot."

Indeed, he had eaten most of it. But there was a little left at the very bottom of the jar, and he pushed his head right in, and began to lick....

By and by Piglet woke up. As soon as he woke he said to himself, "Oh!" Then he said bravely, "Yes," and then, still more bravely, "Quite so." But he didn't feel very brave, for the word which was really jiggeting about in his brain was "Heffalumps."

What was a Heffalump like? Was it Fierce? *Did* it come when you whistled? And *how* did it come? Was it Fond of Pigs at all?

If it was Fond of Pigs, did it make any difference *what sort of Pig*?

Supposing it was Fierce with Pigs, would it make any difference *if the Pig had a grandfather called* TRESPASSERS WILLIAM?

He didn't know the answer to any of these questions...and he was going to see his first Heffalump in about an hour from now!

Of course Pooh would be with him, and it was much more Friendly with two. But suppose Heffalumps were Very Fierce with Pigs *and* Bears? Wouldn't it be better to pretend that he had a headache, and couldn't go up to the Six Pine Trees this morning? But then suppose that it was a very fine day, and there was no Heffalump in the trap, here he would be, in bed all the morning, simply wasting his time for nothing. What should he do?

And then he had a Clever Idea. He would go up very quietly to the Six Pine Trees now, peep very cautiously into the Trap, and see if there was a Heffalump there. And if there was, he would go back to bed, and if there wasn't, he wouldn't.

So off he went. At first he thought that there wouldn't be a Heffalump in the Trap, and then he thought that there would, and as he got nearer he was *sure* that there would, because he could hear it heffalumping about it like anything.

"Oh, dear, oh, dear, oh, dear!" said Piglet to himself. And he wanted to run away. But somehow, having got so near, he felt that he must just see what a Heffalump was like. So he crept to the side of the Trap and looked in....

And all the time Winnie-the-Pooh had been trying to get the honey-jar off his head. The more he shook it, the more tightly it stuck. *"Bother!"* he said, inside the jar, and *"Oh, help!"* and, mostly, *"Ow!"* And he tried bumping it against things, but as he couldn't see what he was bumping it against, it didn't help him; and he tried to climb out of the Trap, but as he could see nothing but jar, and not much of that, he couldn't find his way. So at last he lifted up his head, jar and all, and made a loud, roaring noise of Sadness and Despair...and it was at that moment that Piglet looked down.

"Help, help!" cried Piglet, "a Heffalump, a Horrible Heffalump!" and he scampered off as hard as he could, still crying out, "Help, help, a Herrible Hoffalump! Hoff, Hoff, a Hellible Horralump!

Holl, Holl, a Hoffable Hellerump!" And he didn't stop crying and scampering until he got to Christopher Robin's house.

"Whatever's the matter, Piglet?" said Christopher Robin, who was just getting up.

"Heff," said Piglet, breathing so hard that he could hardly speak, "a Heff—a Heff—a Heffalump."

"Where?"

"Up there," said Piglet, waving his paw.

"What did it look like?"

"Like—like— It had the biggest head you ever saw, Christopher Robin. A great enormous thing, like—like nothing. A huge big—well, like a—I don't know—like an enormous big nothing. Like a jar."

"Well," said Christopher Robin, putting on his shoes, "I shall go and look at it. Come on."

Piglet wasn't afraid if he had Christopher Robin with him, so off they went....

"I can hear it, can't you?" said Piglet anxiously, as they got near.

"I can hear *something*," said Christopher Robin.

It was Pooh bumping his head against a tree-root he had found.
ドンとぶつける　　　　　　　　　　　木の根

"There!" said Piglet. "Isn't it awful?" And he
こわい
held on tight to Christopher Robin's hand.
つかまった

Suddenly Christopher Robin began to laugh... and he laughed...and he laughed...and he laughed. And while he was still laughing—Crash went the
ガッチャーン
Heffalump's head against the tree-root, Smash
割れた
went the jar, and out came Pooh's head again....

Then Piglet saw what a Foolish Piglet he had been, and he was so ashamed of himself that he
恥ずかしい
ran straight off home and went to bed with a
まっすぐに
headache. But Christopher Robin and Pooh went home to breakfast together.

"Oh, Bear!" said Christopher Robin. "How I do love you!"

"So do I," said Pooh.

CHAPTER VI

In Which
Eeyore Has a Birthday
and Gets Two Presents

Eeyore, the old grey Donkey, stood by the side of the stream, and looked at himself in the water.

"Pathetic," he said. "That's what it is. Pathetic."

He turned and walked slowly down the stream for twenty yards, splashed across it, and walked slowly back on the other side. Then he looked at himself in the water again.

"As I thought," he said. "No better from *this* side. But nobody minds. Nobody cares. Pathetic, that's what it is."

There was a crackling noise in the bracken behind him, and out came Pooh.

"Good morning, Eeyore," said Pooh.

"Good morning, Pooh Bear," said Eeyore gloomily. "If it *is* a good morning," he said. "Which I doubt," said he.

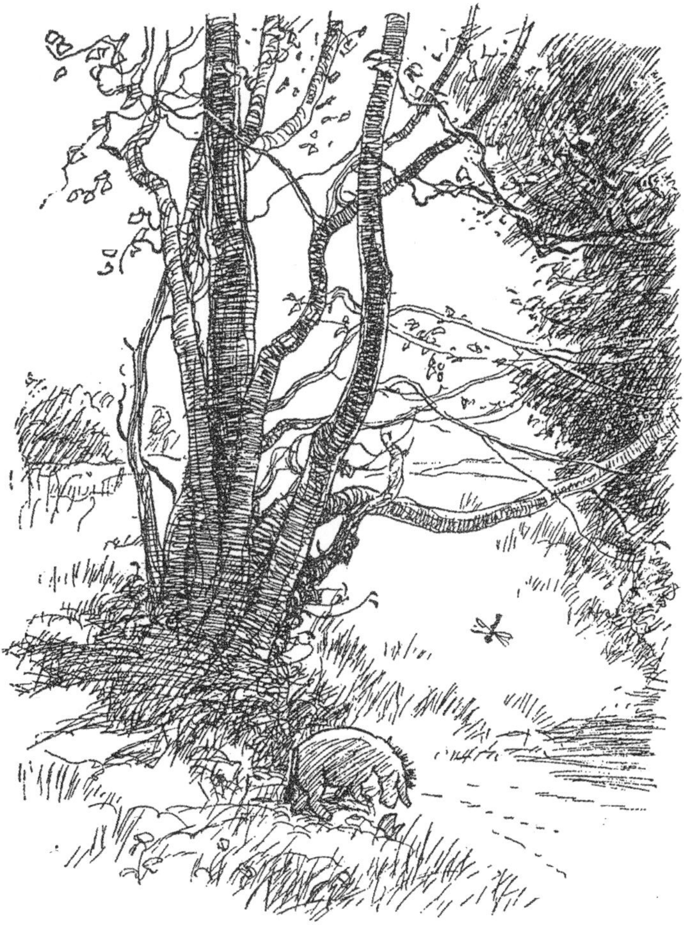

"Why, what's the matter?"

"Nothing, Pooh Bear, nothing. We can't all, and some of us don't. That's all there is to it."

"Can't all *what*?" said Pooh, rubbing his nose.

"Gaiety. Song-and-dance. Here we go round the mulberry bush."

"Oh!" said Pooh. He thought for a long time, and then asked, "What mulberry bush is that?"

"Bon-hommy," went on Eeyore gloomily. "French word meaning bonhommy," he explained. "I'm not complaining, but There It Is."

Pooh sat down on a large stone, and tried to think this out. It sounded to him like a riddle, and he was never much good at riddles, being a Bear of Very Little Brain. So he sang *Cottleston Pie* instead:

> Cottleston, Cottleston, Cottleston Pie,
> A fly can't bird, but a bird can fly.
> Ask me a riddle and I reply:
> *"Cottleston, Cottleston, Cottleston Pie."*

That was the first verse. When he had finished it, Eeyore didn't actually say that he didn't like it, so Pooh very kindly sang the second verse to him:

> Cottleston, Cottleston, Cottleston Pie,
> A fish can't whistle and neither can I.
> Ask me a riddle and I reply:
> "Cottleston, Cottleston, Cottleston Pie."

Eeyore still said nothing at all, so Pooh hummed the third verse quietly to himself:

> Cottleston, Cottleston, Cottleston Pie,
> Why does a chicken, I don't know why.
> Ask me a riddle and I reply:
> "Cottleston, Cottleston, Cottleston Pie."

"That's right," said Eeyore. "Sing. Umty-tiddly, umty-too. Here we go gathering Nuts and May. Enjoy yourself."

"I am," said Pooh.

"Some can," said Eeyore.

"Why, what's the matter?"

"*Is* anything the matter?"

"You seem so sad, Eeyore."

"Sad? Why should I be sad? It's my birthday. The happiest day of the year."

"Your birthday?" said Pooh in great surprise.

"Of course it is. Can't you see? Look at all the presents I have had." He waved a foot from side to side. "Look at the birthday cake. Candles and pink sugar."

Pooh looked—first to the right and then to the left.

"Presents?" said Pooh. "Birthday cake?" said Pooh. "*Where?*"

"Can't you see them?"

"No," said Pooh.

"Neither can I," said Eeyore. "Joke," he explained. "Ha ha!"

Pooh scratched his head, being a little puzzled by all this.

"But is it really your birthday?" he asked.

"It is."

"Oh! Well, Many happy returns of the day, Eeyore."

"And many happy returns to you, Pooh Bear."

"But it isn't *my* birthday."

"No, it's mine."

"But you said 'Many happy returns'—"

"Well, why not? You don't always want to be miserable on my birthday, do you?"

"Oh, I see," said Pooh.

"It's bad enough," said Eeyore, almost breaking down, "being miserable myself, what with no presents and no cake and no candles, and no proper notice taken of me at all, but if everybody else is going to be miserable too—"

This was too much for Pooh. "Stay there!" he called to Eeyore, as he turned and hurried back home as quick as he could; for he felt that he must get poor Eeyore a present of some sort at once, and he could always think of a proper one afterwards.

Outside his house he found Piglet, jumping up and down trying to reach the knocker.

"Hallo, Piglet," he said.

"Hallo, Pooh," said Piglet.

"What are *you* trying to do?"

"I was trying to reach the knocker," said Piglet. "I just came round—"

"Let me do it for you," said Pooh kindly. So he reached up and knocked at the door. "I have just seen Eeyore," he began, "and poor Eeyore is in a Very Sad Condition, because it's his birthday, and nobody has taken any notice of it, and he's very Gloomy—you know what Eeyore is— and there he was, and— What a long time whoever lives here is answering this door." And he knocked again.

"But Pooh," said Piglet, "it's your own house!"

"Oh!" said Pooh. "So it is," he said. "Well, let's go in."

So in they went. The first thing Pooh did was to go to the cupboard to see if he had quite a small jar of honey left; and he had, so he took it down.

"I'm giving this to Eeyore," he explained, "as a present. What are *you* going to give?"

"Couldn't I give it too?" said Piglet. "From both of us?"

"No," said Pooh. "That would *not* be a good plan."

"All right, then, I'll give him a balloon. I've got one left from my party. I'll go and get it now, shall I?"

"That, Piglet, is a *very* good idea. It is just what Eeyore wants to cheer him up. Nobody can be uncheered with a balloon."

So off Piglet trotted; and in the other direction went Pooh, with his jar of honey.

It was a warm day, and he had a long way to go. He hadn't gone more than half-way when a sort of funny feeling began to creep all over him. It began at the tip of his nose and trickled all through him and out at the soles of his feet. It was just as if somebody inside him were saying, "Now then, Pooh, time for a little something."

"Dear, dear," said Pooh, "I didn't know it was as late as that." So he sat down and took the top off his jar of honey. "Lucky I brought this with me," he thought. "Many a bear going out on a warm day like this would never have thought of bringing a little something with him." And he began to eat.

"Now let me see," he thought, as he took his last lick of the inside of the jar, "where was I going? Ah, yes, Eeyore." He got up slowly.

And then, suddenly, he remembered. He had eaten Eeyore's birthday present!

"Bother!" said Pooh. "What *shall* I do? I *must* give him *something*."

For a little while he couldn't think of anything. Then he thought: "Well, it's a very nice pot, even if there's no honey in it, and if I washed it clean, and got somebody to write 'A Happy Birthday' on it, Eeyore could keep things in it, which might be Useful. So, as he was just passing the Hundred Acre Wood, he went inside to call on Owl, who lived there.

"Good morning, Owl," he said.

"Good morning, Pooh," said Owl.

"Many happy returns of Eeyore's birthday," said Pooh.

"Oh, is that what it is?"

"What are you giving him, Owl?"

"What are *you* giving him, Pooh?"

"I'm giving him a Useful Pot to Keep Things In, and I wanted to ask you—"

"Is this it?" said Owl, taking it out of Pooh's paw.

"Yes, and I wanted to ask you—"

"Somebody has been keeping honey in it," said Owl.

"You can keep *anything* in it," said Pooh earnestly. "It's Very Useful like that. And I wanted to ask you—"

"You ought to write 'A Happy Birthday' on it."

"*That* was what I wanted to ask you," said Pooh. "Because my spelling is Wobbly. It's good spelling but it Wobbles, and the letters get in the wrong places. Would *you* write 'A Happy Birthday' on it for me?"

"It's a nice pot," said Owl, looking at it all round.

"Couldn't I give it too? From both of us?"

"No," said Pooh. "That would *not* be a good plan. Now I'll just wash it first, and then you can write on it.'

Well, he washed the pot out, and dried it, while Owl licked the end of his pencil, and wondered how to spell "birthday."

"Can you read, Pooh?" he asked a little anxiously. "There's a notice about knocking and ringing outside my door, which Christopher Robin wrote. Could you read it?"

"Christopher Robin told me what it said, and *then* I could."

"Well, I'll tell you what *this* says, and then you'll be able to."

So Owl wrote...and this is what he wrote:

HIPY PAPY BTHUTHDTH THUTHDA
BTHUTHDY.

Pooh looked on admiringly.

"I'm just saying 'A Happy Birthday,'" said Owl carelessly.

"It's a nice long one," said Pooh, very much impressed by it.

"Well, actually, of course, I'm saying 'A Very Happy Birthday with love from Pooh.' Naturally it takes a good deal of pencil to say a long thing like that."

"Oh, I see," said Pooh.

While all this was happening, Piglet had gone back to his own house to get Eeyore's balloon. He held it very tightly against himself, so that it shouldn't blow away, and he ran as fast as he could so as to get to Eeyore before Pooh did; for he thought that he would like to be the first one to give a present, just as if he had thought of it without being told by anybody. And running along, and thinking how pleased Eeyore would be, he didn't look where he was going...and suddenly he put his foot in a rabbit hole, and fell down flat on his face.

BANG!!!???***!!!

Piglet lay there, wondering what had happened. At first he thought that the whole world had blown up; and then he thought that perhaps only the Forest part of it had; and then he thought that perhaps only *he* had, and he was now alone in the moon or somewhere, and would never see Christopher Robin or Pooh or Eeyore again. And then he thought, "Well, even if I'm in the moon, I needn't be face downwards all the time," so he got cautiously up and looked about him.

He was still in the Forest!

"Well, that's funny," he thought. "I wonder what that bang was. I couldn't have made such a noise just falling down. And where's my balloon? And what's that small piece of damp rag doing?"

It was the balloon!

"Oh, dear!" said Piglet. "Oh, dear, oh, dearie, dearie, dear! Well, it's too late now. I can't go back, and I haven't another balloon, and perhaps Eeyore doesn't *like* balloons so *very* much."

So he trotted on, rather sadly now, and down he came to the side of the stream where Eeyore was, and called out to him.

"Good morning, Eeyore," shouted Piglet.

"Good morning, Little Piglet," said Eeyore. "If it *is* a good morning," he said. "Which I doubt," said he. "Not that it matters," he said.

"Many happy returns of the day," said Piglet, having now got closer.

Eeyore stopped looking at himself in the stream, and turned to stare at Piglet.

"Just say that again," he said.

"Many hap—"

"Wait a moment."

Balancing on three legs, he began to bring his fourth leg very cautiously up to his ear. "I did this yesterday," he explained, as he fell down for the third time. "It's quite easy. It's so as I can hear better.... There, that's done it! Now then, what were you saying?" He pushed his ear forward with his hoof.

"Many happy returns of the day," said Piglet again.

"Meaning me?"

"Of course, Eeyore."

"My birthday?"

"Yes."

"Me having a real birthday?"

"Yes, Eeyore, and I've brought you a present."

Eeyore took down his right hoof from his

right ear, turned round, and with great difficulty put up his left hoof.

"I must have that in the other ear," he said. "Now then."

"A present," said Piglet very loudly.

"Meaning me again?"

"Yes."

"My birthday still?"

"Of course, Eeyore."

"Me going on having a real birthday?"

"Yes, Eeyore, and I brought you a balloon."

"*Balloon?*" said Eeyore. "You did say balloon? One of those big coloured things you blow up? Gaiety, song-and-dance, here we are and there we are?"

"Yes, but I'm afraid—I'm very sorry, Eeyore—but when I was running along to bring it to you, I fell down."

"Dear, dear, how unlucky! You ran too fast, I expect. You didn't hurt yourself, Little Piglet?"

"No, but I—I—oh, Eeyore, I burst the balloon!"

There was a very long silence.

"My balloon?" said Eeyore at last.

Piglet nodded.

"My birthday balloon?"

"Yes, Eeyore," said Piglet sniffing a little. "Here it is. With—with many happy returns of the day."

And he gave Eeyore the small piece of damp rag.

"Is this it?" said Eeyore, a little surprised.
Piglet nodded.
"My present?"
Piglet nodded again.
"The balloon?"
"Yes."

"Thank you, Piglet," said Eeyore. "You don't mind my asking," he went on, "but what colour was this balloon when it—when it *was* a balloon?"

"Red."

"I just wondered.... Red," he murmured to himself. "My favourite colour.... How big was it?"

"About as big as me."

"I just wondered.... About as big as Piglet," he said to himself sadly. "My favourite size. Well, well."

Piglet felt very miserable, and didn't know what to say. He was still opening his mouth to begin something, and then deciding that it wasn't any good saying *that*, when he heard a shout from the other side of the river, and there was Pooh.

"Many happy returns of the day," called out Pooh, forgetting that he had said it already.

"Thank you, Pooh, I'm having them," said Eeyore gloomily.

"I've brought you a little present," said Pooh excitedly.

"I've had it," said Eeyore.

Pooh had now splashed across the stream to Eeyore, and Piglet was sitting a little way off, his head in his paws, snuffling to himself.

"It's a Useful Pot," said Pooh. "Here it is. And it's got 'A Very Happy Birthday with love from Pooh' written on it. That's what all that writing is. And it's for putting things in. There!"

When Eeyore saw the pot, he became quite excited.

"Why!" he said. "I believe my Balloon will just go into that Pot!"

"Oh, no, Eeyore," said Pooh. "Balloons are much too big to go into Pots. What you do with a balloon is, you hold the balloon—"

"Not mine," said Eeyore proudly. "Look, Piglet!" And as Piglet looked sorrowfully round, Eeyore picked the balloon up with his teeth, and placed it carefully in the pot; picked it out and put it on the ground; and then picked it up again and put it carefully back.

"So it does!" said Pooh. "It goes in!"

"So it does!" said Piglet. "And it comes out!"

"Doesn't it?" said Eeyore. "It goes in and out like anything."

"I'm very glad," said Pooh happily, "that I

thought of giving you a Useful Pot to put things in."

"I'm very glad," said Piglet happily, "that I thought of giving you Something to put in a Useful Pot."

But Eeyore wasn't listening. He was taking the balloon out, and putting it back again, as happy as could be....

"And didn't *I* give him anything?" asked Christopher Robin sadly.

"Of course you did," I said. "You gave him— don't you remember—a little—a little—"

"I gave him a box of paints to paint things with."

"That was it."

"Why didn't I give it to him in the morning?"

"You were so busy getting his party ready for him. He had a cake with icing on the top, and three candles, and his name in pink sugar, and—"

"Yes, *I* remember," said Christopher Robin.

CHAPTER VII

In Which
Kanga and Baby Roo
Come to the Forest,
and Piglet Has a Bath

Nobody seemed to know where they came from, but there they were in the Forest: Kanga and Baby Roo. When Pooh asked Christopher Robin, "How did they come here?" Christopher Robin said, "In the Usual Way, if you know what I mean, Pooh," and Pooh, who didn't, said "Oh!" Then he nodded his head twice and said, "In the Usual Way. Ah!" Then he went to call upon his friend Piglet to see what *he* thought about it. And at Piglet's house he found Rabbit. So they all talked about it together.

"What I don't like about it is this," said Rabbit. "Here are we—you, Pooh, and you, Piglet, and Me—and suddenly—"

"And Eeyore," said Pooh.

"And Eeyore—and then suddenly—"

"And Owl," said Pooh.

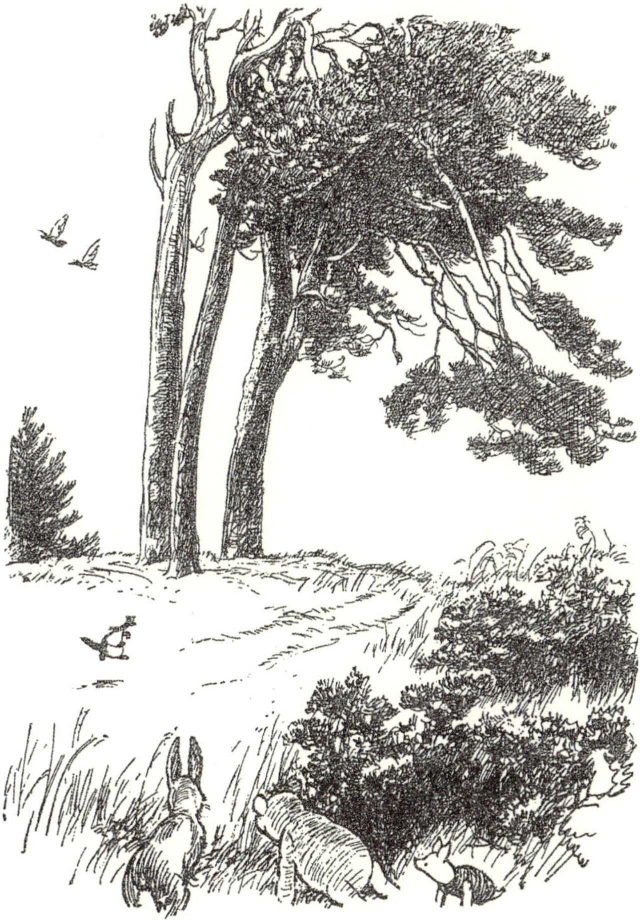

"And Owl—and then all of a sudden—"

"Oh, and Eeyore," said Pooh. "I was forgetting *him*."

"Here—we—are," said Rabbit very slowly and carefully, "all—of—us, and then, suddenly, we wake up one morning, and what do we find? We find a Strange Animal among us. An animal of whom we have never even heard before! An animal who carries her family about with her in her pocket! Suppose *I* carried *my* family about with me in my pocket, how many pockets should I want?"

"Sixteen," said Piglet.

"Seventeen, isn't it?" said Rabbit. "And one more for a handkerchief—that's eighteen. Eighteen pockets in one suit! I haven't time."

There was a long and thoughtful silence...and then Pooh, who had been frowning very hard for some minutes, said: "*I* make it fifteen."

"What?" said Rabbit.

"Fifteen."

"Fifteen what?"

"Your family."

"What about them?"

Pooh rubbed his nose and said that he thought Rabbit had been talking about his family.

"Did I?" said Rabbit carelessly.

"Yes, you said—"

"Never mind, Pooh," said Piglet impatiently.

"The question is, What are we to do about Kanga?"

"Oh, I see," said Pooh.

"The best way," said Rabbit, "would be this. The best way would be to steal Baby Roo and hide him, and then when Kanga says, 'Where's Baby Roo?' we say, '*Aha!*'"

"*Aha!*" said Pooh, practising. "*Aha! Aha!*... Of course," he went on, "we could say '*Aha!*' even if we hadn't stolen Baby Roo."

"Pooh," said Rabbit kindly, "you haven't any brain."

"I know," said Pooh humbly.

"We say '*Aha!*' so that Kanga knows that we know where Baby Roo is. '*Aha!*' means 'We'll tell you where Baby Roo is, if you promise to go away from the Forest and never come back.' Now don't talk while I think."

Pooh went into a corner and tried saying "Aha!" in that sort of voice. Sometimes it seemed to him that it did mean what Rabbit said, and sometimes it seemed to him that it didn't. "I suppose it's just practice," he thought. "I wonder if Kanga will have to practise too so as to understand it."

"There's just one thing," said Piglet, fidgeting a bit. "I was talking to Christopher Robin, and he said that a Kanga was Generally Regarded as One of the Fiercer Animals. I am not frightened of Fierce Animals in the ordinary way, but it is well known that, if One of the Fiercer Animals is Deprived of Its Young, it becomes as fierce as Two of the Fiercer Animals. In which case *'Aha!'* is perhaps a *foolish* thing to say."

"Piglet," said Rabbit, taking out a pencil, and licking the end of it, "you haven't any pluck."

"It is hard to be brave," said Piglet, sniffing slightly, "when you're only a Very Small Animal."

Rabbit, who had begun to write very busily, looked up and said:

"It is because you are a very small animal that you will be Useful in the adventure before us."

Piglet was so excited at the idea of being Useful that he forgot to be frightened any more, and when Rabbit went on to say that Kangas were only Fierce during the winter months, being at other times of an Affectionate Disposition, he could hardly sit still, he was so eager to begin being useful at once.

"What about me?" said Pooh sadly. "I suppose *I* shan't be useful?"

"Never mind, Pooh," said Piglet comfortingly. "Another time perhaps."

"Without Pooh," said Rabbit solemnly as he sharpened his pencil, "the adventure would be impossible."

"Oh!" said Piglet, and tried not to look disappointed. But Pooh went into a corner of the room and said proudly to himself, "Impossible without Me! *That* sort of Bear."

"Now listen all of you," said Rabbit when he had finished writing, and Pooh and Piglet sat listening very eagerly with their mouths open. This was what Rabbit read out:

PLAN TO CAPTURE BABY ROO
1. *General Remarks.* Kanga runs faster than any of Us, even Me.
2. *More General Remarks.* Kanga never takes her eye off Baby Roo, except when he's safely buttoned up in her pocket.
3. *Therefore.* If we are to capture Baby Roo, we must get a Long Start, because Kanga runs faster than any of Us, even Me. (*See* 1.)
4. *A Thought.* If Roo had jumped out of Kanga's pocket and Piglet had jumped in, Kanga wouldn't know the difference, because Piglet

is a Very Small Animal.
5. Like Roo.
6. But Kanga would have to be looking the other way first, so as not to see Piglet jumping in.
7. See 2.
8. *Another Thought*. But if Pooh was talking to her very excitedly, she *might* look the other way for a moment.
9. And then I could run away with Roo.
10. Quickly.
11. *And Kanga wouldn't discover the difference until Afterwards.*

Well, Rabbit read this out proudly, and for a little while after he had read it nobody said anything. And then Piglet, who had been opening and shutting his mouth without making any noise, managed to say very huskily:
"And—Afterwards?"

"How do you mean?"

"When Kanga *does* Discover the Difference?"

"Then we all say '*Aha!*'"

"All three of us?"

"Yes."

"Oh!"

"Why, what's the trouble, Piglet?"

"Nothing," said Piglet, "as long as *we all three* say it. As long as we all three say it," said Piglet, "I don't mind," he said, "but I shouldn't care to say '*Aha!*' by myself. It wouldn't sound nearly so well. By the way," he said, "you *are* quite sure about what you said about the winter months?"

"The winter months?"

"Yes, only being Fierce in the Winter Months."

"Oh, yes, yes, that's all right. Well, Pooh? You see what you have to do?"

"No," said Pooh Bear. "Not yet," he said. "What *do* I do?"

"Well, you just have to talk very hard to Kanga so as she doesn't notice anything."

"Oh! What about?"

"Anything you like."

"You mean like telling her a little bit of poetry or something?"

"That's it," said Rabbit. "Splendid. Now come along."

So they all went out to look for Kanga.

Kanga and Roo were spending a quiet afternoon in a sandy part of the Forest. Baby Roo was practising very small jumps in the sand, and falling down mouse-holes and climbing out of them, and Kanga was fidgeting about and saying "Just one more jump, dear, and then we must go home." And at that moment who should come stumping up the hill but Pooh.

"Good afternoon, Kanga."

"Good afternoon, Pooh."

"Look at me jumping," squeaked Roo, and fell into another mouse-hole.

"Hallo, Roo, my little fellow!"

"We were just going home," said Kanga. "Good afternoon, Rabbit. Good afternoon, Piglet."

Rabbit and Piglet, who had now come up from the other side of the hill, said, "Good afternoon," and "Hallo, Roo," and Roo asked them to look at him jumping, so they stayed and looked.

And Kanga looked too....

"Oh, Kanga," said Pooh, after Rabbit had winked at him twice, "I don't know if you are interested in Poetry at all?"

"Hardly at all," said Kanga.

"Oh!" said Pooh.

"Roo, dear, just one more jump and then we must go home."

There was a short silence while Roo fell down another mouse-hole.

"Go on," said Rabbit in a loud whisper behind his paw.

"Talking of Poetry," said Pooh, "I made up a little piece as I was coming along. It went like this. Er—now let me see—"

"Fancy!" said Kanga. "Now Roo, dear—"

"You'll like this piece of poetry," said Rabbit.

"You'll love it," said Piglet.

"You must listen very carefully," said Rabbit.

"So as not to miss any of it," said Piglet.

"Oh, yes," said Kanga, but she still looked at Baby Roo.

"*How* did it go, Pooh?" said Rabbit.

Pooh gave a little cough and began.

LINES WRITTEN BY A BEAR
OF VERY LITTLE BRAIN

On Monday, when the sun is hot
I wonder to myself a lot:
"Now is it true, or is it not,
"That what is which and which is what?"

On Tuesday, when it hails and snows,
_{ヒョウが降る}
The feeling on me grows and grows
That hardly anybody knows
If those are these or these are those.

On Wednesday, when the sky is blue,
And I have nothing else to do,
I sometimes wonder if it's true
That who is what and what is who.

On Thursday, when it starts to freeze
_{こごえる}
And hoar-frost twinkles on the trees,
_霜　　_{キラキラする}
How very readily one sees
_{すぐに}
That these are whose—but whose are these?

On Friday—

"Yes, it is, isn't it?" said Kanga, not waiting to hear what happened on Friday. "Just one more jump, Roo, dear, and then we really *must* be going."

Rabbit gave Pooh a hurrying-up sort of nudge.

"Talking of Poetry," said Pooh quickly, "have you ever noticed that tree right over there?"

"Where?" said Kanga. "Now, Roo—"

"Right over there," said Pooh, pointing behind Kanga's back.

"No," said Kanga. "Now jump in, Roo, dear, and we'll go home."

"You ought to look at that tree right over there," said Rabbit. "Shall I lift you in, Roo?" And he picked up Roo in his paws.

"I can see a bird in it from here," said Pooh. "Or is it a fish?"

"You ought to see that bird from here," said Rabbit. "Unless it's a fish."

"It isn't a fish, it's a bird," said Piglet.

"So it is," said Rabbit.

"Is it a starling or a blackbird?" said Pooh.

"That's the whole question," said Rabbit. "Is it a blackbird or a starling?"

And then at last Kanga did turn her head to look. And the moment that her head was turned, Rabbit said in a loud voice "In you go, Roo!" and in jumped Piglet into Kanga's pocket, and off scampered Rabbit, with Roo in his paws, as fast as he could.

"Why, where's Rabbit?" said Kanga, turning round again. "Are you all right, Roo, dear?"

Piglet made a squeaky Roo-noise from the bottom of Kanga's pocket.

"Rabbit had to go away," said Pooh. "I think he thought of something he had to go and see about suddenly."

"And Piglet?"

"I think Piglet thought of something at the same time. Suddenly."

"Well, we must be getting home," said Kanga. "Good-bye, Pooh." And in three large jumps she was gone.

Pooh looked after her as she went.

"I wish I could jump like that," he thought. "Some can and some can't. That's how it is."

But there were moments when Piglet wished that Kanga couldn't. Often, when he had had a long walk home through the Forest, he had wished that he were a bird; but now he thought jerkily to himself at the bottom of Kanga's pocket,

"If this is shall flying I take really never to it."

And as he went up in the air, he said, "*Ooooooo!*" and as he came down he said, "*Ow!*"

And he was saying, "*Ooooooo-ow, Ooooooo-ow, Ooooooo-ow*" all the way to Kanga's house.

Of course as soon as Kanga unbuttoned her pocket, she saw what had happened. Just for a moment, she thought she was frightened, and then she knew she wasn't; for she felt quite sure that Christopher Robin would never let any harm happen to Roo. So she said to herself, "If they are having a joke with me, I will have a joke with them."

"Now then, Roo, dear," she said, as she took Piglet out of her pocket. "Bed-time."

"*Aha!*" said Piglet, as well as he could after his Terrifying Journey. But it wasn't a very good "*Aha!*" and Kanga didn't seem to understand what it meant.

"Bath first," said Kanga in a cheerful voice.

"*Aha!*" said Piglet again, looking round anxiously for the others. But the others weren't there. Rabbit was playing with Baby Roo in his own house, and feeling more fond of him every minute, and Pooh, who had decided to be a Kanga, was still at the sandy place on the top of the Forest, practising jumps.

"I am not at all sure," said Kanga in a thoughtful voice, "that it wouldn't be a good idea to have a *cold* bath this evening. Would you like that, Roo, dear?"

Piglet, who had never been really fond of baths, shuddered a long indignant shudder, and said in as brave a voice as he could:

"Kanga, I see that the time has come to speak plainly."

"Funny little Roo," said Kanga, as she got the bath-water ready.

"I am *not* Roo," said Piglet loudly. "I am Piglet!"

"Yes, dear, yes," said Kanga soothingly. "And imitating Piglet's voice too! So clever of him," she went on, as she took a large bar of yellow soap out of the cupboard. "What *will* he be doing next?"

"Can't you *see*?" shouted Piglet. "Haven't you got *eyes*? *Look* at me!"

"I *am* looking, Roo, dear," said Kanga rather severely. "And you know what I told you yesterday about making faces. If you go on making faces like Piglet's, you will grow up to *look* like Piglet—and *then* think how sorry you will be. Now then, into the bath, and don't let me have to speak to you about it again."

Before he knew where he was, Piglet was in the bath, and Kanga was scrubbing him firmly with a large lathery flannel.

"*Ow!*" cried Piglet. "Let me out! I'm Piglet!"

"Don't open the mouth, dear, or the soap goes in," said Kanga. "There! What did I tell you?"

"You—you—you did it on purpose," spluttered Piglet, as soon as he could speak again ...and then accidentally had another mouthful of lathery flannel.

"That's right, dear, don't say anything," said Kanga, and in another minute Piglet was out of the bath, and being rubbed dry with a towel.

"Now," said Kanga, "there's your medicine, and then bed."

"W–w–what medicine?" said Piglet.

"To make you grow big and strong, dear. You don't want to grow up small and weak like Piglet, do you? Well, then!"

At that moment there was a knock at the door.

"Come in," said Kanga, and in came Christopher Robin.

"Christopher Robin, Christopher Robin!" cried Piglet. "Tell Kanga who I am! She keeps saying I'm Roo. I'm *not* Roo, am I?"

Christopher Robin looked at him very carefully, and shook his head.

"You can't be Roo," he said, "because I've just seen Roo playing in Rabbit's house."

"Well!" said Kanga. "Fancy that! Fancy my making a mistake like that."

"There you are!" said Piglet. "I told you so. I'm Piglet."

Christopher Robin shook his head again.

"Oh, you're not Piglet," he said. "I know Piglet well, and he's *quite* a different colour."

Piglet began to say that this was because he had just had a bath, and then he thought that perhaps he wouldn't say that, and as he opened his mouth to say something else, Kanga slipped the medicine spoon in, and then patted him on the back and told him that it was really quite a nice taste when you got used to it.

"I knew it wasn't Piglet," said Kanga. "I wonder who it can be."

"Perhaps it's some relation of Pooh's," said Christopher Robin. "What about a nephew or an uncle or something?"

Kanga agreed that this was probably what it was, and said that they would have to call it by some name.

"I shall call it Pootel," said Christopher Robin. "Henry Pootel for short."

And just when it was decided, Henry Pootel wriggled out of Kanga's arms and jumped to the ground. To his great joy Christopher Robin had left the door open. Never had Henry Pootel Piglet run so fast as he ran then, and he didn't stop running until he had got quite close to his house. But when he was a hundred yards away he stopped running, and rolled the rest of the way home, so as to get his own nice comfortable colour again....

So Kanga and Roo stayed in the Forest. And every Tuesday Roo spent the day with his great friend Rabbit, and every Tuesday Kanga spent the day with her great friend Pooh, teaching him to jump, and every Tuesday Piglet spent the day with his great friend Christopher Robin. So they were all happy again.

CHAPTER VIII

In Which
Christopher Robin
Leads an Expotition
to the North Pole

One fine day Pooh had stumped up to the top of the Forest to see if his friend Christopher Robin was interested in Bears at all. At breakfast that morning (a simple meal of marmalade spread lightly over a honeycomb or two) he had suddenly thought of a new song. It began like this:

"Sing Ho! for the life of a Bear!"

When he had got as far as this, he scratched his head, and thought to himself, "That's a very good start for a song, but what about the second line?" He tried singing "Ho," two or three times, but it didn't seem to help. "Perhaps it would be better," he thought, "if I sang Hi for the life of a Bear." So he sang it...but it wasn't. "Very well, then," he said, "I shall sing that first line twice, and perhaps if I sing it very quickly, I shall find myself singing the third and fourth lines before I have time to think of them, and that will be a Good Song. Now then":

> Sing Ho! for the life of a Bear!
> Sing Ho! for the life of a Bear!
> I don't much mind if it rains or snows,
> 'Cos I've got a lot of honey on my nice new nose,
> I don't much care if it snows or thaws,
> 'Cos I've got a lot of honey on my nice clean paws!
> Sing Ho! for a Bear!
> Sing Ho! for a Pooh!
> And I'll have a little something in an hour or two!

He was so pleased with this song that he sang it all the way to the top of the Forest, "and if I go on singing it much longer," he thought, "it will be time for the little something, and then the last line won't be true. So he turned it into a hum instead.

Christopher Robin was sitting outside his door, putting on his Big Boots. As soon as he saw the Big Boots, Pooh knew that an Adventure was going to happen, and he brushed the honey off his nose with the back of his paw, and spruced himself up as well as he could, so as to look Ready for Anything.

"Good morning, Christopher Robin," he called out.

"Hallo, Pooh Bear. I can't get this boot on."

"That's bad," said Pooh.

"Do you think you could very kindly lean against me, 'cos I keep pulling so hard that I fall over backwards."

Pooh sat down, dug his feet into the ground, and pushed hard against Christopher Robin's back, and Christopher Robin pushed hard against his, and pulled and pulled at his boot until he had got it on.

"And that's that," said Pooh. "What do we do next?"

"We are all going on an Expedition," said Christopher Robin, as he got up and brushed himself. "Thank you, Pooh."

"Going on an Expotition?" said Pooh eagerly. "I don't think I've ever been on one of those. Where are we going to on this Expotition?"

"Expedition, silly old Bear. It's got an 'x' in it."

"Oh!" said Pooh. "I know." But he didn't really.

"We're going to discover the North Pole."

"Oh!" said Pooh again. "What *is* the North Pole?" he asked.

"It's just a thing you discover," said Christopher Robin carelessly, not being quite sure himself.

"Oh! I see," said Pooh. "Are bears any good at discovering it?"

"Of course they are. And Rabbit and Kanga and all of you. It's an Expedition. That's what an Expedition means. A long line of everybody. You'd better tell the others to get ready, while I see if my gun's all right. And we must all bring Provisions."

"Bring what?"

"Things to eat."

"Oh!" said Pooh happily. "I thought you said Provisions. I'll go and tell them." And he stumped off.

The first person he met was Rabbit.

"Hallo, Rabbit," he said, "is that you?"

"Let's pretend it isn't," said Rabbit, "and see what happens."

"I've got a message for you."

"I'll give it to him."

"We're all going on an Expotition with Christopher Robin!"

"What is it when we're on it?"

"A sort of boat, I think," said Pooh.

"Oh! that sort."

"Yes. And we're going to discover a Pole or something. Or was it a Mole? Anyhow we're going to discover it."

"We are, are we?" said Rabbit.

"Yes. And we've got to bring Pro-things to eat with us. In case we want to eat them. Now I'm going down to Piglet's. Tell Kanga, will you?"

He left Rabbit and hurried down to Piglet's house. The Piglet was sitting on the ground at the door of his house blowing happily at a dandelion, and wondering whether it would be this year, next year, sometime, or never. He had just discovered that it would be never, and was trying to remember what "*it*" was, and hoping it wasn't anything nice, when Pooh came up.

"Oh! Piglet," said Pooh excitedly, "we're going on an Expotition, all of us, with things to eat. To discover something."

"To discover what?" said Piglet anxiously.

"Oh! just something."

"Nothing fierce?"

"Christopher Robin didn't say anything about fierce. He just said it had an 'x'."

"It isn't their necks I mind," said Piglet earnestly. "It's their teeth. But if Christopher Robin is coming I don't mind anything."

In a little while they were all ready at the top of the Forest, and the Expotition started. First came Christopher Robin and Rabbit, then Piglet and Pooh; then Kanga, with Roo in her pocket, and Owl; then Eeyore; and, at the end, in a long line, all Rabbit's friends-and-relations.

"I didn't ask them," explained Rabbit carelessly. "They just came. They always do. They can march at the end, after Eeyore."

"What I say," said Eeyore, "is that it's unsettling. I didn't want to come on this Expo—what Pooh said. I only came to oblige. But here I am; and if I am the end of the Expo—what we're talking about—then let me *be* the end. But if, every time I want to sit down for a little rest, I have to brush away half a dozen of Rabbit's smaller friends-and-relations first, then this isn't an Expo—whatever it is—at all, it's simply a Confused Noise. That's what *I* say."

"I see what Eeyore means," said Owl. "If you ask me—"

"I'm not asking anybody," said Eeyore. "I'm just telling everybody. We can look for the North Pole, or we can play 'Here we go gathering Nuts and May' with the end part of an ant's nest. It's all the same to me."

There was a shout from the top of the line.

"Come on!" called Christopher Robin.

"Come on!" called Pooh and Piglet.

"Come on!" called Owl.

"We're starting," said Rabbit. "I must go." And he hurried off to the front of the Expotition with Christopher Robin.

"All right," said Eeyore. "We're going. Only Don't Blame Me."

So off they all went to discover the Pole. And as they walked, they chattered to each other of this and that, all except Pooh, who was making up a song.

"This is the first verse," he said to Piglet, when he was ready with it.

"First verse of what?"

"My song."

"What song?"

"This one."

"Which one?"

"Well, if you listen, Piglet, you'll hear it."

"How do you know I'm not listening?"

Pooh couldn't answer that one, so he began to sing.

> They all went off to discover the Pole,
>> Owl and Piglet and Rabbit and all;
> It's a Thing you Discover, as I've been tole
>> By Owl and Piglet and Rabbit and all.
> Eeyore, Christopher Robin and Pooh
> And Rabbit's relations all went too—
> And where the Pole was none of them knew....
>> Sing Hey! for Owl and Rabbit and all!

"Hush!" said Christopher Robin turning round to Pooh, "we're just coming to a Dangerous Place."

"Hush!" said Pooh turning round quickly to Piglet.

"Hush!" said Piglet to Kanga.

"Hush!" said Kanga to Owl, while Roo said "Hush!" several times to himself very quietly.

"Hush!" said Owl to Eeyore.

"*Hush!*" said Eeyore in a terrible voice to all Rabbit's friends-and-relations, and "Hush!" they said hastily to each other all down the line, until it got to the last one of all. And the last and smallest friend-and-relation was so upset to find that the whole Expotition was saying "Hush!" to *him*, that he buried himself head downwards in a crack in the ground, and stayed there for two days until

the danger was over, and then went home in a great hurry, and lived quietly with his Aunt ever-afterwards. His name was Alexander Beetle.

They had come to a stream which twisted and tumbled between high rocky banks, and Christopher Robin saw at once how dangerous it was.

"It's just the place," he explained, "for an Ambush."

"What sort of bush?" whispered Pooh to Piglet. "A gorse-bush?"

"My dear Pooh," said Owl in his superior way, "don't you know what an Ambush is?"

"Owl," said Piglet, looking round at him

severely, "Pooh's whisper was a perfectly private whisper, and there was no need—"

"An Ambush," said Owl, "is a sort of Surprise."

"So is a gorse-bush sometimes," said Pooh.

"An Ambush, as I was about to explain to Pooh," said Piglet, "is a sort of Surprise."

"If people jump out at you suddenly, that's an Ambush," said Owl.

"It's an Ambush, Pooh, when people jump at you suddenly," explained Piglet.

Pooh, who now knew what an Ambush was, said that a gorse-bush had sprung at him suddenly one day when he fell off a tree, and he had taken six days to get all the prickles out of himself.

"We are not *talking* about gorse-bushes," said Owl a little crossly.

"I am," said Pooh.

They were climbing very cautiously up the stream now, going from rock to rock, and after they had gone a little way they came to a place where the banks widened out at each side, so that on each side of the water there was a level strip of grass on which they could sit down and rest. As soon as he saw this, Christopher Robin called "Halt!" and they all sat down and rested.

"I think," said Christopher Robin, "that we ought to eat all our Provisions now, so that we shan't have so much to carry."

"Eat all our what?" said Pooh.

"All that we've brought," said Piglet, getting to work.

"That's a good idea," said Pooh, and he got to work too.

"Have you all got something?" asked Christopher Robin with his mouth full.

"All except me," said Eeyore. "As Usual." He looked round at them in his melancholy way. "I suppose none of you are sitting on a thistle by any chance?"

"I believe I am," said Pooh "Ow!" He got up, and looked behind him. "Yes, I was. I thought so."

"Thank you, Pooh. If you've quite finished with it." He moved across to Pooh's place, and began to eat.

"It dosen't do them any Good, you know, sitting on them," he went on, as he looked up munching. "Takes all the Life out of them. Remember that another time, all of you. A little Considera-

tion, a little Thought for Others, makes all the difference.
いくばり

As soon as he had finished his lunch Christopher Robin whispered to Rabbit, and Rabbit said, "Yes, yes, of course," and they walked a little way up the stream together.

"I didn't want the others to hear," said Christopher Robin.

"Quite so," said Rabbit, looking important.

"It's—I wondered— It's only—Rabbit, I suppose *you* don't know, What does the North Pole look like?"

"Well," said Rabbit, stroking his whiskers. "Now you're asking me."
がてこ　　　　　　　　　　　ひげ

"I did know once, only I've sort of forgotten," said Christopher Robin carelessly.

"It's a funny thing," said Rabbit, "but I've sort of forgotten too, although I did know *once*."

"I suppose it's just a pole stuck in the ground?"
ささった

"Sure to be a pole," said Rabbit, "because of calling it a pole, and if it's a pole, well, I should think it would be sticking in the ground, shouldn't you, because there'd be nowhere else to stick it."

"Yes, that's what I thought."

"The only thing," said Rabbit, "is, *where is it sticking?*"

"That's what we're looking for," said Christopher Robin.

They went back to the others. Piglet was lying on his back, sleeping peacefully. Roo was washing his face and paws in the stream, while Kanga explained to everybody proudly that this was the first time he had ever washed his face himself, and Owl was telling Kanga an Interesting Anecdote full of long words like Encyclopædia and Rhododendron to which Kanga wasn't listening.

"I don't hold with all this washing," grumbled Eeyore. "This modern Behind-the-ears nonsense. What do *you* think, Pooh?"

"Well," said Pooh, "*I* think—"

But we shall never know what Pooh thought, for there came a sudden squeak from Roo, a splash, and a loud cry of alarm from Kanga.

"So much for *washing*," said Eeyore.

"Roo's fallen in!" cried Rabbit, and he and Christopher Robin came rushing down to the rescue.

"Look at me swimming!" squeaked Roo from the middle of his pool, and was hurried down a waterfall into the next pool.

"Are you all right, Roo, dear?" called Kanga anxiously.

"Yes!" said Roo. "Look at me sw—" and down he went over the next waterfall into another pool.

Everybody was doing something to help. Piglet, wide awake suddenly, was jumping up and down and making "Oo, I say" noises; Owl was explaining that in a case of Sudden and Temporary Immersion the Important Thing was to keep the Head Above Water; Kanga was jumping along the bank, saying "Are you *sure* you're all right, Roo, dear?" to which Roo, from whatever pool he was in at the moment, was answering "Look at me swimming!" Eeyore had turned round and hung his tail over the first pool into which Roo fell, and with his back to the accident was grumbling quietly to himself, and saying, "All this washing; but catch on to my tail, little Roo, and you'll be all right"; and Christopher Robin and Rabbit came hurrying past Eeyore, and were calling out to the others in front of them.

"All right, Roo, I'm coming," called Christopher Robin.

"Get something across the stream lower down, some of you fellows," called Rabbit.

But Pooh was getting something. Two pools below Roo he was standing with a long pole in his paws, and Kanga came up and took one end of it, and between them they held it across the lower part of the pool; and Roo, still bubbling proudly, "Look at me swimming," drifted up against it, and climbed out.

"Did you see me swimming?" squeaked Roo excitedly, while Kanga scolded him and rubbed him down. "Pooh, did you see me swimming? That's called swimming, what I was doing. Rabbit, did you see what I was doing? Swimming. Hallo, Piglet! I say, Piglet! What do you think I was doing? Swimming! Christopher Robin, did you see me—"

But Christopher Robin wasn't listening. He was looking at Pooh.

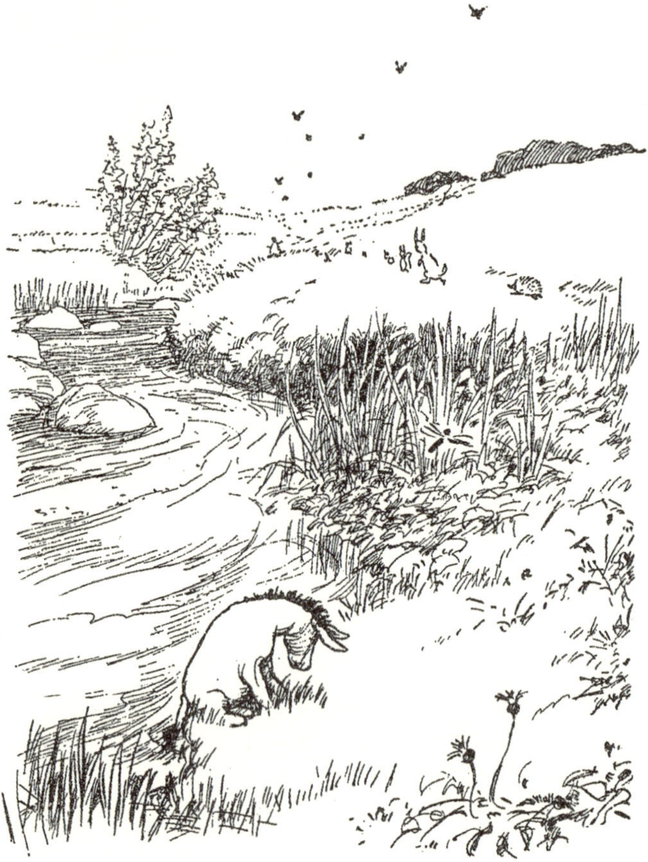

"Pooh," he said, "where did you find that pole?"

Pooh looked at the pole in his hands.

"I just found it," he said. "I thought it ought to be useful. I just picked it up."

"Pooh," said Christopher Robin solemnly, "the Expedition is over. You have found the North Pole!"

"Oh!" said Pooh.

Eeyore was sitting with his tail in the water when they all got back to him.

"Tell Roo to be quick, somebody," he said. "My tail's getting cold. I don't want to mention it, but I just mention it. I don't want to complain, but there it is. My tail's cold."

"Here I am!" squeaked Roo.

"Oh, there you are."

"Did you see me swimming?"

Eeyore took his tail out of the water, and swished it from side to side.

"As I expected," he said. "Lost all feeling. Numbed it. That's what it's done. Numbed it. Well, as long as nobody minds, I suppose it's all right."

"Poor old Eeyore. I'll dry it for you," said Christopher Robin, and he took out his handkerchief and rubbed it up.

"Thank you, Christopher Robin. You're the only one who seems to understand about tails.

They don't think—that's what's the matter with some of these others. They've no imagination. A tail isn't a tail to *them*, it's just a Little Bit Extra at the back."

"Never mind, Eeyore," said Christopher Robin, rubbing his hardest. "Is *that* better?"

"It's feeling more like a tail perhaps. It Belongs again, if you know what I mean."

"Hullo, Eeyore," said Pooh, coming up to them with his pole.

"Hullo, Pooh. Thank you for asking, but I shall be able to use it again in a day or two."

"Use what?" said Pooh.

"What we are talking about."

"I wasn't talking about anything," said Pooh, looking puzzled.

"My mistake again. I thought you were saying how sorry you were about my tail, being all numb, and could you do anything to help?"

"No," said Pooh. "That wasn't me," he said. He thought for a little and then suggested helpfully, "Perhaps it was somebody else."

"Well, thank him for me when you see him."

Pooh looked anxiously at Christopher Robin.

"Pooh's found the North Pole," said Christopher Robin. "Isn't that lovely?"

Pooh looked modestly down.

"Is that it?" said Eeyore.

"Yes," said Christopher Robin.

"Is that what we were looking for?"

"Yes," said Pooh.

"Oh!" said Eeyore. "Well, anyhow—it didn't rain," he said.

They stuck the pole in the ground, and Christopher Robin tied a message on to it.

NORTH POLE

DISCOVERED BY POOH

POOH FOUND IT.

Then they all went home again. And I think, but I am not quite sure, that Roo had a hot bath and went straight to bed. But Pooh went back to his own house, and feeling very proud of what he had done, had a little something to revive himself.
　　　　　　　　ひとくち食べる　　　　　　　　元気づける

CHAPTER IX

In Which
Piglet Is Entirely Surrounded
by Water

It rained and it rained and it rained. Piglet told himself that never in all his life, and *he* was goodness knows *how* old—three, was it, or four? —never had he seen so much rain. Days and days and days.

"If only," he thought, as he looked out of the window, "I had been in Pooh's house, or Christopher Robin's house, or Rabbit's house when it began to rain, then I should have had Company all this time, instead of being here all alone, with nothing to do except wonder when it will stop." And he imagined himself with Pooh, saying, "Did you ever see such rain, Pooh?" and Pooh saying, "Isn't it awful, Piglet?" and Piglet saying, "I wonder how it is over Christopher Robin's way," and Pooh saying, "I should think poor old Rabbit is about flooded out by this time." It would have been jolly to talk like this, and really, it wasn't much good having anything exciting like floods, if you couldn't share them with somebody.

For it was rather exciting. The little dry ditches in which Piglet had nosed about so often had become streams, the little streams across which he had splashed were rivers, and the river, between whose steep banks they had played so happily, had sprawled out of its own bed and was taking up so much room everywhere, that Piglet was beginning to wonder whether it would be coming into *his* bed soon.

"It's a little Anxious," he said to himself, "to be a Very Small Animal Entirely Surrounded by Water. Christopher Robin and Pooh could escape by Climbing Trees, and Kanga could escape by Jumping, and Rabbit could escape by Burrowing, and Owl could escape by Flying, and Eeyore could escape by—by Making a Loud Noise Until Rescued, and here am I, surrounded by water and I can't do *anything*."

It went on raining, and every day the water got a little higher, until now it was nearly up to Piglet's window…and still he hadn't done anything.

"There's Pooh," he thought to himself. "Pooh hasn't much Brain, but he never comes to any harm. He does silly things and they turn out right.

There's Owl. Owl hasn't exactly got Brain, but he Knows Things. He would know the Right Thing to Do when Surrounded by Water. There's Rabbit. He hasn't Learnt in Books, but he can always Think of a Clever Plan. There's Kanga. She isn't

Clever, Kanga isn't, but she would be so anxious about Roo that she would do a Good Thing to Do without thinking about it. And then there's Eeyore. And Eeyore is so miserable anyhow that he wouldn't mind about this. But I wonder what Christopher Robin would do?"

Then suddenly he remembered a story which Christopher Robin had told him about a man on a desert island who had written something in a bottle and thrown it in the sea; and Piglet thought that if he wrote something in a bottle and threw it in the water, perhaps somebody would come and rescue *him*!

He left the window and began to search his house, all of it that wasn't under water, and at last he found a pencil and a small piece of dry paper, and a bottle with a cork to it. And he wrote on one side of the paper:

HELP!
PIGLIT (ME)

and on the other side:

IT'S ME PIGLIT, HELP HELP.

Then he put the paper in the bottle, and he corked the bottle up as tightly as he could, and he

leant out of his window as far as he could lean
without falling in, and he threw the bottle as far
as he could throw—*splash!*—and in a little while
it bobbed up again on the water; and he watched
it floating slowly away in the distance, until his
eyes ached with looking, and sometimes he thought
it was the bottle, and sometimes he thought it was
just a ripple on the water which he was follow-
ing, and then suddenly he knew that he would
never see it again and that he had done all that
he could do to save himself.

"So now," he thought, "somebody else will
have to do something, and I hope they will do it
soon, because if they don't I shall have to swim,
which I can't, so I hope they do it soon." And then
he gave a very long sigh and said, "I wish Pooh
were here. It's so much more friendly with two."

When the rain began Pooh was asleep. It rained,
and it rained, and it rained, and he slept and he
slept and he slept. He had had a tiring day. You

remember how he discovered the North Pole; well, he was so proud of this that he asked Christopher Robin if there were any other Poles such as a Bear of Little Brain might discover.

"There's a South Pole," said Christopher Robin, "and I expect there's an East Pole and a West Pole, though people don't like talking about them."

Pooh was very excited when he heard this, and suggested that they should have an Expotition to discover the East Pole, but Christopher Robin had thought of something else to do with Kanga; so Pooh went out to discover the East Pole by himself. Whether he discovered it or not, I forget; but he was so tired when he got home that, in the very middle of his supper, after he had been eating for little more than half-an-hour, he fell fast asleep in his chair, and slept and slept and slept.

Then suddenly he was dreaming. He was at the East Pole, and it was a very cold pole with the coldest sort of snow and ice all over it. He had found a beehive to sleep in, but there wasn't room for his legs, so he had left them outside. And Wild Woozles, such as inhabit the East Pole, came and nibbled all the fur off his legs to make nests for their Young. And the more they nibbled, the colder his legs got, until suddenly he woke up with an *Ow!*—and there he was, sitting in his chair with his feet in the water, and water all round him!

He splashed to his door and looked out....

"This is Serious," said Pooh. "I must have an Escape."

So he took his largest pot of honey and escaped with it to a broad branch of his tree, well above the water, and then he climbed down again and escaped with another pot...and when the whole Escape was finished, there was Pooh sitting on his branch, dangling his legs, and there, beside him, were ten pots of honey....

Two days later, there was Pooh, sitting on his branch, dangling his legs, and there, beside him, were four pots of honey.

Three days later, there was Pooh, sitting on his

branch, dangling his legs, and there, beside him, was one pot of honey.

Four days later, there was Pooh…

And it was on the morning of the fourth day that Piglet's bottle came floating past him, and with one loud cry of "Honey!" Pooh plunged into the water, seized the bottle, and struggled back to his tree again.

"Bother!" said Pooh, as he opened it. "All that wet for nothing. What's that bit of paper doing?"

He took it out and looked at it.

"It's a Missage," he said to himself, "that's what it is. And that letter is a 'P,' and so is that, and so is that, and 'P' means 'Pooh,' so it's a very important Missage to me, and I can't read it. I must find Christopher Robin or Owl or Piglet, one of those Clever Readers who can read things, and they will tell me what this missage means. Only I can't swim. Bother!"

Then he had an idea, and I think that for a Bear of Very Little Brain, it was a good idea. He said to himself:

"If a bottle can float, then a jar can float, and if a jar floats, I can sit on the top of it, if it's a very big jar."

So he took his biggest jar, and corked it up. "All boats have to have a name," he said, "so I shall call mine *The Floating Bear*." And with these words he dropped his boat into the water and jumped in after it.

For a little while Pooh and *The Floating Bear* were uncertain as to which of them was meant to be on the top,

but after trying one or two different positions, they settled down with *The Floating Bear* under-

neath and Pooh triumphantly astride it, paddling
vigorously with his feet.

Christopher Robin lived at the very top of the Forest. It rained, and it rained, and it rained, but the water couldn't come up to *his* house. It was rather jolly to look down into the valleys and see the water all round him, but it rained so hard that he stayed indoors most of the time, and thought about things. Every morning he went out with his umbrella and put a stick in the place where the water came up to, and every next morning he went out and couldn't see his stick any more, so he put another stick in the place where the water came up to, and then he walked home again, and each morning he had a shorter way to walk than he had had the morning before. On the morning of the fifth day he saw the water all round him, and knew that for the first time in his life he was on a real island. Which was very exciting.

It was on this morning that Owl came flying over the water to say "How do you do?" to his friend Christopher Robin.

"I say, Owl," said Christopher Robin, "isn't this fun? I'm on an island!"

"The atmospheric conditions have been very unfavourable lately," said Owl.

"The what?"

"It has been raining," explained Owl.

"Yes," said Christopher Robin. "It has."

"The flood-level has reached an unprecedented height."

"The who?"

"There's a lot of water about," explained Owl.

"Yes," said Christopher Robin, "there is."

"However, the prospects are rapidly becoming more favourable. At any moment—"

"Have you seen Pooh?"

"No. At any moment—"

"I hope he's all right," said Christopher Robin. "I've been wondering about him. I expect Piglet's with him. Do you think they're all right, Owl?"

"I expect so. You see, at any moment—"

"Do go and see, Owl. Because Pooh hasn't got very much brain, and he might do something silly, and I do love him so, Owl. Do you see, Owl?"

"That's all right," said Owl. "I'll go. Back directly." And he flew off.

In a little while he was back again.

"Pooh isn't there," he said.

"Not there?"

"Has *been* there. He's been sitting on a branch of his tree outside his house with nine pots of honey. But he isn't there now."

"Oh, Pooh!" cried Christopher Robin. "Where *are* you?"

"Here I am," said a growly voice behind him. "Pooh!"

They rushed into each other's arms.

"How did you get here, Pooh?" asked Christopher Robin, when he was ready to talk again.

"On my boat," said Pooh proudly. "I had a Very Important Missage sent me in a bottle, and owing to having got some water in my eyes, I couldn't read it, so I brought it to you. On my boat."

With these proud words he gave Christopher Robin the missage.

"But it's from Piglet!" cried Christopher Robin when he had read it.

"Isn't there anything about Pooh in it?" asked Bear, looking over his shoulder.

Christopher Robin read the message aloud.

"Oh, are those 'P's' Piglets? I thought they were Poohs."

"We must rescue him at once! I thought he was with *you*, Pooh. Owl, could you rescue him on your back?"

"I don't think so," said Owl, after grave thought. "It is doubtful if the necessary dorsal muscles—"

"Then would you fly to him at *once* and say that Rescue is Coming? And Pooh and I will think of a Rescue and come as quick as ever we can. Oh, don't *talk*, Owl, go on quick!" And, still thinking of something to say, Owl flew off.

"Now then, Pooh," said Christopher Robin, "where's your boat?"

"I ought to say," explained Pooh as they walked down to the shore of the island, "that it isn't just an ordinary sort of boat. Sometimes it's a Boat, and sometimes it's more of an Accident. It all depends."

"Depends on what?"

"On whether I'm on the top of it or underneath it."

"Oh! Well, where is it?"

"There!" said Pooh, pointing proudly to *The Floating Bear*.

It wasn't what Christopher Robin expected, and the more he looked at it, the more he thought what a Brave and Clever Bear Pooh was, and the more Christopher Robin thought this, the more Pooh looked modestly down his nose and tried to pretend he wasn't.

"But it's too small for two of us," said Christopher Robin sadly.

"Three of us with Piglet."

"That makes it smaller still. Oh, Pooh Bear, what shall we do?"

And then this Bear, Pooh Bear, Winnie-the-Pooh, F.O.P. (Friend of Piglet's), R.C. (Rabbit's Companion), P.D. (Pole Discoverer), E.C. and T.F. (Eeyore's Comforter and Tail-finder)—in fact, Pooh himself—said something so clever that Christopher Robin could only look at him with mouth open and eyes staring, wondering if this was really the Bear of Very Little Brain whom he had known and loved so long.

"We might go in your umbrella," said Pooh.

"?"

"We might go in your umbrella," said Pooh.

"??"

"We might go in your umbrella," said Pooh.

"!!!!!!"

For suddenly Christopher Robin saw that they might. He opened his umbrella and put it point downwards in the water. It floated but wobbled. Pooh got in. He was just beginning to say that it was all right now, when he found that it wasn't, so after a short drink which he didn't really want he waded back to Christopher Robin. Then they both got in together, and it wobbled no longer.

"I shall call this boat *The Brain of Pooh*," said Christopher Robin, and *The Brain of Pooh* set sail forthwith in a south-westerly direction, revolving gracefully.

You can imagine Piglet's joy when at last the ship came in sight of him. In after-years he liked to think that he had been in Very Great Danger during the Terrible Flood, but the only danger he had really been in was in the last half-hour of his imprisonment, when Owl, who had just flown up, sat on a branch of his tree to comfort him, and told him a very long story about an aunt who had once laid a seagull's egg by mistake, and the story went on and on, rather like this sentence, until Piglet, who was listening out of his window without much hope, went to sleep quietly and naturally, slipping slowly out of the window towards the water until he was only hanging on by his toes, at which moment luckily, a sudden loud squawk from Owl, which was really part of the story, being what his aunt said, woke the Piglet up and just gave him time to jerk himself back into safety and say, "How interesting, and did she?" when —well, you can imagine his joy when at last he saw the good ship *The Brain of Pooh* (*Captain*, C. Robin; *1st Mate*, P. Bear) coming over the sea to rescue him.

And that is really the end of the story, and as I am very tired after that last sentence, I think I shall stop there.

CHAPTER X

In Which
Christopher Robin
Gives Pooh a Party,
and We Say Good-Bye

One day when the sun had come back over the Forest, bringing with it the scent of May, and all the streams of the Forest were tinkling happily to find themselves their own pretty shape again, and the little pools lay dreaming of the life they had seen and the big things they had done, and in the warmth and quiet of the Forest the cuckoo was trying over his voice carefully and listening to see if he liked it, and wood-pigeons were complaining gently to themselves in their lazy comfortable way that it was the other fellow's fault, but it didn't matter very much; on such a day as this Christopher Robin whistled in a special way he had, and Owl came flying out of the Hundred Acre Wood to see what was wanted.

"Owl," said Christopher Robin, "I am going to give a party."

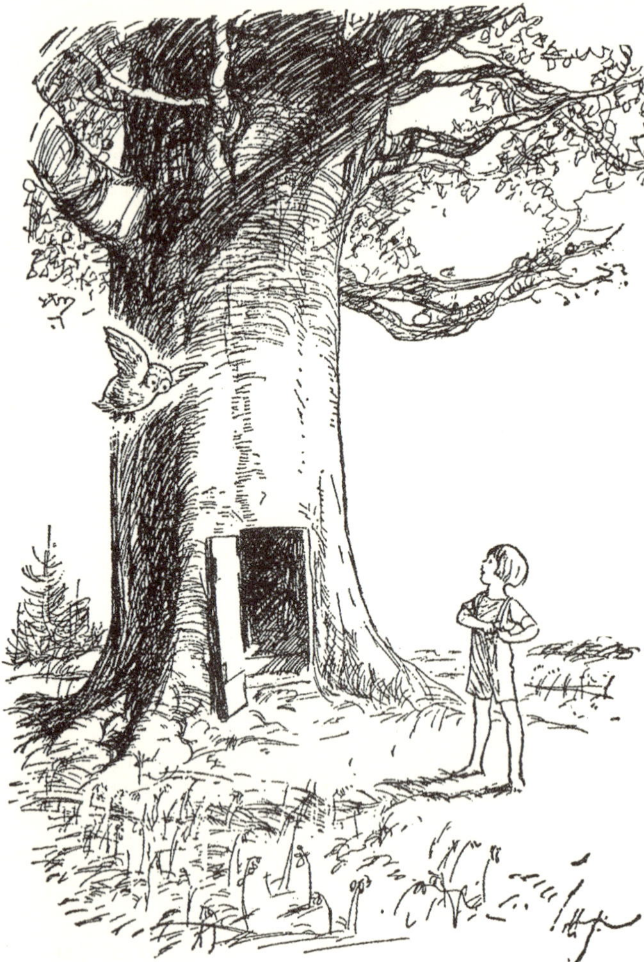

"You are, are you?" said Owl.

"And it's to be a special sort of party, because it's because of what Pooh did when he did what he did to save Piglet from the flood."

"Oh, that's what it's for, is it?" said Owl.

"Yes, so will you tell Pooh as quickly as you can, and all the others, because it will be tomorrow."

"Oh, it will, will it?" said Owl, still being as helpful as possible.

"So will you go and tell them, Owl?"

Owl tried to think of something very wise to say, but couldn't, so he flew off to tell the others. And the first person he told was Pooh.

"Pooh," he said, "Christopher Robin is giving a party."

"Oh!" said Pooh. And then, seeing that Owl expected him to say something else, he said, "Will there be those little cake things with pink sugar icing?"

Owl felt that it was rather beneath him to talk about little cake things with pink sugar icing, so he told Pooh exactly what Christopher Robin had said, and flew off to Eeyore.

"A party for Me?" thought Pooh to himself. "How grand!" And he began to wonder if all the other animals would know that it was a special Pooh Party, and if Christopher Robin had told them about *The Floating Bear* and *The Brain of Pooh*

and all the wonderful ships he had invented and
sailed on, and he began to think how awful it
would be if everybody had forgotten about it, and
nobody quite knew what the party was for; and
the more he thought like this, the more the party
got muddled in his mind, like a dream when nothing goes right.

And the dream began to sing itself over in his
head until it became a sort of song. It was an

ANXIOUS POOH SONG

3 Cheers for Pooh!
(*For Who?*)
For Pooh—
(*Why what did he do?*)
I thought you knew;
He saved his friend from a wetting!
3 Cheers for Bear!
(*For where?*)
For Bear—
He couldn't swim,
But he rescued him!

(*He rescued who?*)
Oh, listen, do!
I am talking of Pooh—
(*Of who?*)
Of Pooh!
(*I'm sorry I keep forgetting.*)
Well, Pooh was a Bear of Enormous Brain
<small>大きな</small>
(*Just say it again!*)
Of enormous brain—
(*Of enormous what?*)
Well, he ate a lot,
And I don't know if he could swim or not,
But he managed to float
On a sort of boat
(*On a sort of what?*)
Well, a sort of pot—
So now let's give him three hearty cheers
<small>心からの</small>
(*So now let's give him three hearty whiches?*)
And hope he'll be with us for years and years,
And grow in health and wisdom and riches!
3 Cheers for Pooh!
(*For who?*)
For Pooh—
3 Cheers for Bear!
(*For where?*)
For Bear—
3 Cheers for the wonderful Winnie-the-Pooh!
(*Just tell me, somebody*—WHAT DID HE DO?)

While this was going on inside him, Owl was talking to Eeyore.

"Eeyore," said Owl, "Christopher Robin is giving a party."

"Very interesting," said Eeyore. "I suppose they will be sending me down the odd bits which got trodden on. Kind and Thoughtful. Not at all, don't mention it."

"There is an Invitation for you."
"What's that like?"
"An Invitation!"

"Yes, I heard you. Who dropped it?"

"This isn't anything to eat, it's asking you to the party. To-morrow."

Eeyore shook his head slowly.

"You mean Piglet. The little fellow with the excited ears. That's Piglet. I'll tell him."

"No, no!" said Owl, getting quite fussy. "It's you!"

"Are you sure?"

"Of course I'm sure. Christopher Robin said 'All of them! Tell all of them.'"

"All of them, except Eeyore?"

"All of them," said Owl sulkily.

"Ah!" said Eeyore. "A mistake, no doubt, but still I shall come. Only don't blame *me* if it rains."

But it didn't rain. Christopher Robin had made a long table out of some long pieces of wood, and they all sat around it. Christopher Robin sat at one end, and Pooh sat at the other, and between them on one side were Owl and Eeyore and Piglet, and between them on the other side were Rabbit, and Roo and Kanga. And all Rabbit's friends-and-relations spread themselves about on the grass, and waited hopefully in case anybody spoke to them, or dropped anything, or asked them the time.

It was the first party to which Roo had ever been, and he was very excited. As soon as ever they had sat down he began to talk.

"Hallo, Pooh!" he squeaked.

"Hallo, Roo!" said Pooh.

Roo jumped up and down in his seat for a little while and then began again.

"Hallo, Piglet!" he squeaked.

Piglet waved a paw at him, being too busy to say anything.

"Hallo, Eeyore!" said Roo.

Eeyore nodded gloomily at him. "It will rain soon, you see if it doesn't," he said.

Roo looked to see if it didn't, and it didn't, so he said, "Hallo, Owl!"—and Owl said, "Hallo, my little fellow," in a kindly way, and went on telling Christopher Robin about an accident which had nearly happened to a friend of his whom Christopher Robin didn't know, and Kanga said to Roo, "Drink up your milk first, dear, and talk afterwards."

So Roo, who was drinking his milk, tried to say that he could do both at once…and had to be patted on the back and dried for quite a long time afterwards.

When they had all nearly eaten enough, Christopher Robin banged on the table with his spoon, and everybody stopped talking and was very silent, except Roo who was just finishing a loud attack of hiccups and trying to look as if it was one of Rabbit's relations.

"This party," said Christopher Robin, "is a party because of what someone did, and we all know who it was, and it's his party, because of what he did, and I've got a present for him and here it is." Then he felt about a little and whispered, "Where is it?"

While he was looking, Eeyore coughed in an impressive way and began to speak.

"Friends," he said, "including oddments, it is a great pleasure, or perhaps I had better say it has been a pleasure so far, to see you at my party. What I did was nothing. Any of you—except Rabbit and Owl and Kanga—would have done the same. Oh, and Pooh. My remarks do not, of course, apply to Piglet and Roo, because they are too small. Any of you would have done the same. But it just happened to be Me. It was not, I need hardly say, with an idea of getting what Christopher Robin is looking for now"—and he put his front leg to his mouth and said in a loud whisper, "Try under the table"—"that I did what I did—but because I feel that we should all do what we can to help. I feel that we should all—"

"H—hup!" said Roo accidentally.

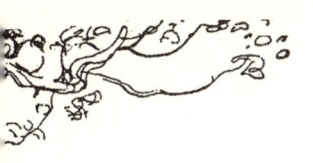

"Roo, dear!" said Kanga reproachfully.
"Was it me?" asked Roo, a little surprised.
"What's Eeyore talking about?" Piglet whispered to Pooh.

"I don't know," said Pooh rather dolefully.

"I thought this was *your* party."

"I thought it was *once*. But I suppose it isn't."

"I'd sooner it was yours than Eeyore's," said Piglet.

"So would I," said Pooh.

"H—hup!" said Roo again.

"AS—I—WAS—SAYING," said Eeyore loudly and sternly, "as I was saying when I was interrupted by various Loud Sounds, I feel that—"

"Here it is!" cried Christopher Robin excitedly. "Pass it down to silly old Pooh. It's for Pooh."

"For Pooh?" said Eeyore.

"Of course it is. The best bear in all the world."

"I might have known," said Eeyore. "After all, one can't complain. I have my friends. Somebody spoke to me only yesterday. And was it last week or the week before that Rabbit bumped into me and said 'Bother!' The Social Round. Always something going on."

Nobody was listening, for they were all saying, "Open it, Pooh," "What is it, Pooh?" "I know what it is," "No, you don't," and other helpful remarks of this sort. And of course Pooh was opening it as quickly as ever he could, but without cutting the string, because you never know when a bit of string might be Useful. At last it was undone.

When Pooh saw what it was, he nearly fell down, he was so pleased. It was a Special Pencil Case. There were pencils in it marked "B" for Bear, and pencils marked "HB" for Helping Bear, and pencils marked "BB" for Brave Bear. There was a knife for sharpening the pencils, and india-rubber for rubbing out anything which you had spelt wrong, and a ruler for ruling lines for the words to walk on, and inches marked on the ruler in case you wanted to know how many inches anything was, and Blue Pencils and Red Pencils and Green Pencils for saying special things in blue and red and green. And all these lovely things were in little pockets of their own in a Special Case which shut with a click when you clicked it. And they were all for Pooh.

"Oh!" said Pooh.

"Oh, Pooh!" said everybody else except Eeyore.

"Thank-you," growled Pooh.

But Eeyore was saying to himself, "This writing business. Pencils and what-not. Over-rated, if you ask me. Silly stuff. Nothing in it."

Later on, when they had all said "Good-bye" and "Thank-you" to Christopher Robin, Pooh and Piglet walked home thoughtfully together in the golden evening, and for a long time they were silent.

"When you wake up in the morning, Pooh," said Piglet at last, "what's the first thing you say to yourself?"

"What's for breakfast?" said Pooh. "What do *you* say, Piglet?"

"I say, I wonder what's going to happen exciting *today*?" said Piglet.

Pooh nodded thoughtfully.

"It's the same thing," he said.

* * *

"And what did happen?" asked Christopher Robin.

"When?"

"Next morning."

"I don't know."

"Could you think and tell me and Pooh sometime?"

"If you wanted it very much."

"Pooh does," said Christopher Robin.

He gave a deep sigh, picked his bear up by the leg and walked off to the door, trailing Winnie-the-Pooh behind him. At the door he turned and said "Coming to see me have my bath?"

"I might," I said.

"Was Pooh's pencil case any better than mine?"

"It was just about the same," I said.

He nodded and went out...and in a moment I heard Winnie-the-Pooh—*bump, bump, bump*—going up the stairs behind him.

クマのプーさん
Winnie-the-Pooh

2001年9月21日	第1刷発行
2003年4月11日	第5刷発行

著 者	A. A. ミルン
さしえ	E. H. シェパード
発行者	畑野文夫
発行所	講談社インターナショナル株式会社
	〒112-8652 東京都文京区音羽 1-17-14
	電話 03-3944-6493(編集部)
	03-3944-6492(営業部・業務部)
	ホームページ http://www.kodansha-intl.co.jp
印刷所	図書印刷株式会社
製本所	図書印刷株式会社

落丁本、乱丁本は購入書店名を明記のうえ、講談社インターナショナル業務部宛にお送りください。送料小社負担にてお取替えいたします。なお、この本についてのお問い合わせは、編集部宛にお願いいたします。本書の無断複写(コピー)は著作権法上での例外を除き、禁じられています。

定価はカバーに表示してあります。

© A. A. Milne and E. H. Shepard 1954
© 講談社インターナショナル株式会社 2001
Printed in Japan

ISBN4-7700-2474-6

あなたの英語が変わる
講談社パワー・イングリッシュ
ネイティブチェック済

ホームページ http://www.kodansha-intl.co.jp

これを英語で言えますか?
学校で教えてくれない身近な英単語

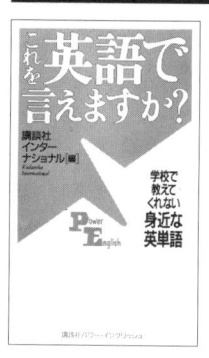

「腕立てふせ」、「○×式テスト」、「短縮ダイヤル」、「$a^2+b^3=c^4$」……あなたはこのうちいくつを英語で言えますか?
日本人英語の盲点になっている英単語に、70強のジャンルから迫ります。読んでみれば、「なーんだ、こんなやさしい単語だったのか」、「そうか、こう言えば良かったのか」と思いあたる単語や表現がいっぱいです。
雑学も満載しましたので、忘れていた単語が生き返ってくるだけでなく、覚えたことが記憶に残ります。弱点克服のボキャビルに最適です。

講談社インターナショナル 編　232ページ
ISBN 4-7700-2132-1

続・これを英語で言えますか?
面白くって止まらない英文&英単語

「英語」って、こんなに楽しいものだった!
「知らなかったけど、知りたかった…」、「言ってみたかったけど、言えなかった…」、本書は、そんな日本人英語の盲点に、70もの分野から迫ります。
「自然現象」「動・植物名」から「コンピュータ用語」や「経済・IT用語」、さらには「犬のしつけ」「赤ちゃんとの英会話」まで…、雑学も満載しましたので、眠っていた単語が生き返ってきます。
ついでに、「アメリカの50の州名が全部言えるようになっちゃった」、「般若心経って英語の方が分かりやすいわネ」…となれば、あなたはもう英語から離れられなくなることでしょう。英語の楽しさを再発見して下さい。

講談社インターナショナル 編　240ページ
ISBN 4-7700-2833-4

講談社バイリンガル・ブックス

ホームページ　http://www.kodansha-intl.co.jp

英語で読んでも面白い！
- 楽しく読めて自然に英語が身に付く日英対訳表記
- 実用から娯楽まで読者の興味に応える多彩なテーマ
- 重要単語、表現法がひと目で分かる段落対応レイアウト

46判変形 (188 x 113 mm) 仮製

印のタイトルは、英文テキスト部分を録音したカセット・テープが、印のタイトルはCDが発売されています。本との併用により聞く力・話す力を高め、実用的な英語が身につく格好のリスニング教材です。

1　増補改訂第2版 英語で話す「日本」Q&A
　　Talking About Japan *Updated* Q&A

3　英語で折り紙　Origami in English

4　英語で読む日本史　Japanese History: 11 Experts Reflect on the Past

5　ベスト・オブ 宮沢賢治短編集　The Tales of Miyazawa Kenji

7　マザー・グース 愛される唄70選　Mother Goose: 70 Nursery Rhymes

9　ベスト・オブ 窓ぎわのトットちゃん
　　Best of Totto-chan: The Little Girl at the Window

11　英語で話す「日本の謎」Q&A 外国人が聞きたがる100のWHY
　　100 Tough Questions for Japan

12　英語で話す「日本の心」和英辞典では引けないキーワード197
　　Keys to the Japanese Heart and Soul

13　アメリカ日常生活のマナーQ&A　Do As Americans Do

15　英語で日本料理　100 Recipes from Japanese Cooking

16　まんが 日本昔ばなし　Once Upon a Time in Japan

17　改訂第2版 イラスト 日本まるごと事典　Japan at a Glance *Updated*

19　英語で話す「世界」Q&A　Talking About the World Q&A

20　誤解される日本人 外国人がとまどう41の疑問　The Inscrutable Japanese

21　英語で話す「アメリカ」Q&A　Talking About the USA Q&A

22　英語で話す「日本の文化」　Japan as I See It

23　ベスト・オブ・天声人語　VOX POPULI, VOX DEI

24　英語で話す「仏教」Q&A　Talking About Buddhism Q&A

28	茶の本 The Book of Tea
29	まんが 日本昔ばなし 妖しのお話 Once Upon a Time in *Ghostly* Japan
30	武士道 BUSHIDO
35	英語で話す「雑学ニッポン」Q&A Japan Trivia
36	英語で話す日本ビジネスQ&A ここが知りたい、日本のカイシャ Frequently Asked Questions on Corporate Japan
37	英語で話す国際経済Q&A 一目で分かるキーワード図解付き A Bilingual Guide to the World Economy
40	英語で比べる「世界の常識」 Everyday Customs Around the World
43	「英国」おもしろ雑学事典 All You Wanted to Know About the U.K.
45	バイリンガル日本史年表 Chronology of Japanese History
47	英語で「ちょっといい話」スピーチにも使える222のエピソード Bits & Pieces of Happiness
49	英語で話す「医療ハンドブック」 Getting Medical Aid in English
51	「人を動かす」英語の名言 Inspiring Quotations from Around the World
52	英語で「いけばな」 The Book of Ikebana
53	英語で話す「日本の伝統芸能」 The Complete Guide to Traditional Japanese Performing Arts
57	「日本らしさ」を英語にできますか? Japanese Nuance in Plain English!
58-1	全図解 日本のしくみ [政治・経済・司法編] The Complete Illustrated Guide to Japanese Systems
58-2	全図解 日本のしくみ [生活文化・社会・医療・娯楽・スポーツ編] The 100% Complete Illustrated Guide to Japanese Systems
60	英語で話す「キリスト教」Q&A Talking About Christianity Q&A
61	ビジネスで使えることわざ 英会話の香辛料 Proverbs for Business
62	まんが 日本昔ばなし 愉快なお話 Once Upon a Time in JOLLY Japan
63	数字で読む日本人 A Statistical Look at Japan
64	英語で占う「あなたの運勢」 The Future Revealed: The Japanese Way
65	英語で贈るグリーティング・カード Sweet Cards
66	英語で楽しむ日本の家庭料理 Japanese Family-Style Recipes

講談社英語文庫

ホームページ　http://www.kodansha-intl.co.jp

楽しく読んで英語が身につく

- 海外と日本の古典から最新話題作まで、幅広いジャンルの作品が英語で読めます。
- 英語の初心者から上級者まで十分読みごたえのある、さまざまなレベルの作品が揃っています。
- なるべく辞書を使わずに楽しく読めるよう、原則として巻末にNotes (語句の解説)をつけてあります。
- 人気イラストレーターによる美しい装画、さし絵が人気です。
- 比較的大きめの活字を使った、読みやすい英文が好評です。

☆印は英語のレベルを表わしています。☆の数が多くなるほどレベルが上がります。
＊印は、原作をもとに英語文庫のために書き下ろした作品です。

印のタイトルは、英文テキスト部分を録音したカセット・テープが発売されています。シリーズの中から人気作を選りすぐりカセット化しました。通勤・通学、家事の時間など、いつでもどこでも気軽に楽しめます。名作の朗読を聴くことにより、耳を英語に慣らすことができます。

海外の作品

著者	番号	タイトル	カセット	レベル
ステュウット・アットキン	82-1	イギリス昔ばなし＊	◉	☆
イソップ	39	イソップ物語＊	◉	☆
ウィーダ	154	フランダースの犬		☆☆
ジーン・ウェブスター	67	あしながおじさん		☆☆
レイモンド・カーヴァー	45	ぼくが電話をかけている場所		☆☆☆☆
ルース・スタイルス・ガネット	161-1	エルマーのぼうけん		☆☆
	161-2	エルマーとりゅう		☆☆
	161-3	エルマーと16ぴきのりゅう		☆☆
トルーマン・カポーティ	64	ティファニーで朝食を	◉	☆☆☆☆
ルイス・キャロル	40-1	ふしぎの国のアリス	◉	☆☆
	40-2	鏡の国のアリス		☆☆
ボブ・グリーン	50-1	チーズバーガーズ		☆☆☆☆
	50-2	アメリカン・ビート		☆☆☆☆
アガサ・クリスティ	127-1	アガサ・クリスティ短編集	◉	☆☆☆
	127-2	ポアロの事件簿		☆☆☆
グリム兄弟	94	グリム童話集＊	◉	☆
J・D・サリンジャー	71-1	ライ麦畑でつかまえて		☆☆☆☆
	71-2	ナイン・ストーリーズ		☆☆☆☆
ウイリアム・サローヤン	84	パパ・ユーア クレイジー		☆☆
エリック・シーガル	80	ラブ・ストーリィ		☆☆☆

著者	番号	タイトル	カセット	評価
シェイクスピア	103	ロミオとジュリエット*		☆☆
ジョナサン・スウィフト	157	ガリバー旅行記*		☆☆
R・L・スティーブンソン	166	宝島		☆☆
ヨハンナ・スピリ	156	アルプスの少女ハイジ*		☆☆
ミゲール・デ・セルバンテス	167	ドン・キホーテ		☆☆
チャールズ・ディケンズ	53	クリスマス・キャロル	◉	☆☆
コナン・ドイル	105-1	シャーロック・ホームズの冒険	◉	☆☆☆
マーク・トウェーン	143	トム・ソーヤーの冒険		☆☆
P・L・トラヴァース	83	メアリー・ポピンズ		☆☆
L・フランク・バーム	74	オズの魔法使い	◉	☆☆
ピート・ハミル	58	ニューヨーク・スケッチブック		☆☆☆☆
J・M・バリ	43	ピーター・パン		☆☆
F・スコット・フィッツジェラルド	110	華麗なるギャツビー		☆☆☆☆
アルフ・プリョイセン	171	小さなスプーンおばさん		☆☆
オトフリート・プロイスラー	172	小さい魔女		☆☆
アーネスト・ヘミングウェイ	73	老人と海		☆☆☆
O・ヘンリー	96-1	O・ヘンリー 短編集	◉	☆☆☆
	96-2	O・ヘンリー 名作集		☆☆☆
ルプランス・ド・ボーモン	133	美女と野獣*		☆☆
マイケル・ボンド	160	くまのパディントン		☆☆
ラルフ・マッカーシー	49	アメリカ昔ばなし*	◉	☆☆
	130	ギリシャ神話*		☆☆
A・A・ミルン	135-1	クマのプーさん	◉	☆☆
	135-2	プー横丁にたった家		☆☆
L・M・モンゴメリ	57-1	赤毛のアン		☆☆☆
トーベ・ヤンソン	138-1	たのしいムーミン一家	◉	☆
	138-2	ムーミン谷の彗星		☆☆
ヴィクトル・ユゴー	170	レ・ミゼラブル		☆☆
C・S・ルイス	169	ライオンと魔女		☆☆
ヒュー・ロフティング	150	ドリトル先生航海記		☆☆
ローラ・インガルス・ワイルダー	60	大草原の小さな家		☆☆
オスカー・ワイルド	75	幸福な王子		☆☆
小林与志 (絵)	7-1	マザー・グース	◉	☆
	7-2	マザー・グース 2		☆

日本の作品

著者	番号	タイトル	評価
秋月りす	112-1	OL進化論	☆☆
	112-2	OL進化論2	☆☆
芥川龍之介	27	蜘蛛の糸	☆☆
天樹征丸 (文) さとうふみや (絵)	129-1	金田一少年の事件簿：オペラ座館・新たなる殺人	☆☆
	129-2	金田一少年の事件簿：電脳山荘殺人事件	☆☆
	129-3	金田一少年の事件簿：上海魚人伝説殺人事件	☆☆
大平光代	174	だから、あなたも生きぬいて	☆☆
川内彩友美 (編)	18-1	まんが日本昔ばなし 1	☆
	18-2	まんが日本昔ばなし 2	☆
	18-3	まんが日本昔ばなし 3	☆
	18-4	まんが日本昔ばなし 4	☆
	18-5	まんが日本昔ばなし 5	☆
	18-6	まんが日本昔ばなし：動物たちのお話	☆
柏葉幸子	28	霧のむこうのふしぎな町	☆☆
黒柳徹子	2	窓ぎわのトットちゃん	☆☆
太宰 治	36	走れメロス	☆☆
夏目漱石	8-1	坊っちゃん [cassette]	☆☆
	8-2	吾輩は猫である	☆☆
新美南吉	114	ごんぎつね	☆
葉月九ロウ (作) 赤松 健 (画)	173-1	ラブひな：混浴厳禁〜ひなた荘のヒミツ	☆☆
	173-2	ラブひな：混浴厳禁〜ひなた旅館へようこそ!	☆☆
林 望	168	イギリスはおいしい	☆☆
星 新一	22-1	きまぐれロボット	☆☆
	22-2	エヌ氏の遊園地	☆☆
松谷みよ子	10	ちいさいモモちゃん	☆
宮沢賢治	31-1	銀河鉄道の夜	☆☆
	31-2	注文の多い料理店	☆☆
	31-3	セロ弾きのゴーシュ	☆☆
村上春樹	26	風の歌を聴け	☆☆☆☆
吉川英治	1	宮本武蔵 名場面集	☆☆☆
ラフカディオ・ハーン	107	怪談	☆☆☆
ラルフ・マッカーシー	153	日本の神話*	☆☆
	162	日本わらい話*	☆☆

講談社ルビー・ブックス

ホームページ　http://www.kodansha-intl.co.jp

「ルビ訳」とは？　「わかりにくい単語・イディオム・言い回しには、ルビ（ふりがな）のように訳がつく」——これが「ルビ訳」です。疑問をその場で解決し、最後までどんどん読み進むことができます。必要なとき以外は本文に集中できるよう、実物では「ルビ訳」の部分が薄いグリーンで印刷されています。　46判変型（188 x 113 mm）仮製

- 文脈がつかみやすく、「飛ばし読み」「中断・再開」してもストーリーが追えます。　● 自分なりの訳が組みたてられ、読解力がつきます。
- 基本的に辞書は不要。短時間で読み終えることができます。

1	ホームズの名推理・ベスト5　コナン・ドイル 著	208ページ	ISBN 4-7700-2370-7
2	老人と海　ヘミングウェイ 著	128ページ	ISBN 4-7700-2373-1
5	金田一少年の事件簿　雷祭 殺人事件 天樹征丸 作　さとうふみや 画	144ページ	ISBN 4-7700-2447-9
6	アルジャーノンに花束を　ダニエル・キイス 著	304ページ	ISBN 4-7700-2372-3
7-①	そして誰もいなくなった　アガサ・クリスティ 著	272ページ	ISBN 4-7700-2547-5
7-②	オリエント急行殺人事件　アガサ・クリスティ 著	272ページ	ISBN 4-7700-2665-X
7-④	アクロイド殺人事件　アガサ・クリスティ 著	304ページ	ISBN 4-7700-2719-2
8-①	緋色の研究　コナン・ドイル 著	192ページ	ISBN 4-7700-2555-6
9	ティファニーで朝食を　トルーマン・カポーティ 著	128ページ	ISBN 4-7700-2377-4
10	ふしぎの国のアリス　ルイス・キャロル 著	176ページ	ISBN 4-7700-2549-1
11	シェイクスピア物語　ラム 著	240ページ	ISBN 4-7700-2559-9
12	あしながおじさん　ジーン・ウェブスター 著	176ページ	ISBN 4-7700-2597-1
14	グリム童話集　グリム兄弟 編	208ページ	ISBN 4-7700-2605-6
15	マディソン郡の橋　ロバート・ウォラー 著	192ページ	ISBN 4-7700-2624-2
17	ベスト・オブ・O・ヘンリー　O・ヘンリー 著	128ページ	ISBN 4-7700-2656-0
21	セブン　アンソニー・ブルーノ 著	256ページ	ISBN 4-7700-2679-X
23	華麗なるギャツビー　フィッツジェラルド 著	208ページ	ISBN 4-7700-2714-1
26	イソップ物語	128ページ	ISBN 4-7700-2691-9
27	アルマゲドン　M・C・ボーリン 著	208ページ	ISBN 4-7700-2425-8
31	アンデルセン童話集　アンデルセン 著	128ページ	ISBN 4-7700-2423-1
32	ジキル博士とハイド氏　R・L・スティーブンソン 著	144ページ	ISBN 4-7700-2419-3
33	クマのプーさん　A・A・ミルン 著	192ページ	ISBN 4-7700-2474-6
34	Yの悲劇　エラリー・クイーン 著	368ページ	ISBN 4-7700-2420-7
35	たのしいムーミン一家　トーベ・ヤンソン 著	192ページ	ISBN 4-7700-2460-6
36	深夜プラス1　ギャビン・ライアル 著	320ページ	ISBN 4-7700-2422-3

風と共に去りぬ（全6巻）　マーガレット・ミッチェル 著

30-①	前編1　224ページ　ISBN 4-7700-2766-4	30-④	後編1　256ページ　ISBN 4-7700-2769-9
30-②	前編2　224ページ　ISBN 4-7700-2767-2	30-⑤	後編2　256ページ　ISBN 4-7700-2770-2
30-③	前編3　352ページ　ISBN 4-7700-2768-0	30-⑥	後編3　288ページ　ISBN 4-7700-2771-0

講談社バイリンガル・コミックス

ホームページ　http://www.kodansha-intl.co.jp

吹き出しのセリフは英語、コマの外にオリジナル版の日本語を添えた画期的レイアウトで、原作のもつ雰囲気と面白さはそのまま。楽しく読みながら英語の勉強になります。

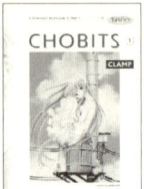

バイリンガル版
ちょびっツ
Chobits
CLAMP 著
第1巻〜第2巻

バイリンガル版
カードキャプターさくら
Cardcaptor Sakuras
CLAMP 著
第1巻〜第6巻

バイリンガル版
金田一少年の事件簿
The New Kindaichi Files
金成陽三郎 原作　さとうふみや 漫画
第1巻 オペラ座館殺人事件
第2巻 異人館村殺人事件
第3巻 雪夜叉伝説殺人事件
第4巻 雪夜叉伝説殺人事件：解決編
天樹征丸 原作　さとうふみや 漫画
天草財宝伝説殺人事件：問題編
天草財宝伝説殺人事件：解答編

バイリンガル版
GTO
Great Teacher Onizuka
藤沢とおる 著
第1巻〜第3巻

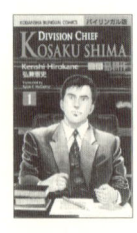

バイリンガル版
部長 島耕作
Division Chief Kosaku Shima
弘兼憲史 著
第1巻〜第5巻

バイリンガル版
ジパング
Zipang
かわぐちかいじ 著
第1巻〜第4巻

バイリンガル版
ゲゲゲの鬼太郎
Ge Ge Ge-no-Kitaro
水木しげる 著
京極夏彦 監修
第1巻〜第3巻

バイリンガル版
リボンの騎士
Princess Knight
手塚治虫 著
第1巻〜第6巻

バイリンガル版
デビルマン
Devilman
永井豪 & ダイナミックプロ 著
第1巻〜第5巻

バイリンガル版
攻殻機動隊
The Ghost In The Shell
士郎正宗 著

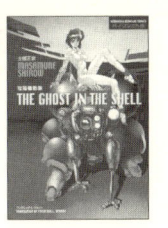

バイリンガル版
あさきゆめみし
The Tale of Genji
大和和紀 著
星の章(上)(下)
花の章(上)(下)

バイリンガル版
ピーチガール
Peach Girl
上田美和 著
第1巻〜第4巻

バイリンガル版
天才バカボン
The Genius Bakabon
赤塚不二夫 著
第1巻〜第3巻

バイリンガル版
ラブひな
Love ♡ Hina
赤松健 著
第1巻〜第8巻
&
ラブひな英語塾
——受験対策版——

対訳
サザエさん
長谷川町子 著
The Wonderful World of Sazae-san
第1巻〜第12巻
全12巻セット

対訳 よりぬき
いじわるばあさん
Granny Mischief
長谷川町子 著
第1巻〜第3巻

対訳
OL進化論
Survival in the Office
秋月りす 著
第1巻〜第5巻
全5巻セット

対訳 よりぬき
コボちゃん
Kobo, the Li'l Rascal
植田まさし 著
第1巻〜第3巻

講談社パワー・イングリッシュ

ホームページ　http://www.kodansha-intl.co.jp

実用英語の総合シリーズ

- 旅行・留学からビジネスまで、コミュニケーションの現場で役立つ「実用性」
- ニューヨーク、ロンドンの各拠点での、ネイティブ チェックにより保証される「信頼性」
- 英語の主要ジャンルを網羅し、目的に応じた本選びができる「総合性」

46判変型、仮製

1-1 これを英語で言えますか？　学校で教えてくれない身近な英単語

講談社インターナショナル 編　　　　　　　　　232ページ　ISBN 4-7700-2132-1

「腕立てふせ」、「○×式テスト」、「短縮ダイヤル」、「$a^2+b^3=c^4$」……あなたはこのうちいくつを英語で言えますか？　日本人英語の盲点になっている英単語に、本書は70強のジャンルから迫ります。読んでみれば、「なーんだ、こんなやさしい単語だったのか」、「そうか、こう言えば良かったのか」と思いあたる単語や表現がいっぱいです。雑学も満載しましたので、忘れていた単語が生き返ってくるだけでなく、覚えたことが記憶に残ります。弱点克服のボキャビルに最適です。

1-2 続・これを英語で言えますか？　面白くって止まらない英文＆英単語

講談社インターナショナル 編　　　　　　　　　240ページ　ISBN 4-7700-2833-4

「英語」って、こんなに楽しいものだった！「知らなかったけど、知りたかった…」、「言ってみたかったけど、言えなかった…」、本書は、そんな日本人英語の盲点に、70もの分野から迫ります。「自然現象」「動・植物名」から「コンピュータ用語」や「経済・IT用語」、さらには「犬のしつけ」「赤ちゃんとの英会話」まで…、雑学も満載しましたので、眠っていた単語が生き返ってきます。ついでに、「アメリカの50の州名が全部言えるようになっちゃった」、「般若心経って英語の方が分かりやすいわネ」…となれば、あなたはもう英語から離れられなくなることでしょう。英語の楽しさを再発見して下さい。

4 ダメ！ その英語［ビジネス編］　日本人英語NG集

連東孝子 著　　　　　　　　　　　　　　　　　176ページ　ISBN 4-7700-2469-X

社長賞をもらった同僚に"You are lucky!"と言ってはダメ！　本書では、ビジネスの場面を中心に、日本人が「誤解した例」、「誤解された例」を110のエピソードを通してご紹介します。本書の随所で、「えっ、この英語なぜいけないの？」「この英語がどうして通じないの？」と気付く自分を発見することでしょう。日本人英語のウイークポイントが克服できます。

5 米語イディオム600　ELTで学ぶ使い分け＆言い替え

バーバラ・ゲインズ 著　　　　　　　　　　　　208ページ　ISBN 4-7700-2461-4

堅苦しくない自然な英語で話したい。これは英語を勉強している人にとって永遠のテーマと言えるのではないでしょうか。そのひとつの答えは英会話でイディオムを自然に使うことです。なかなかイディオムを使いこなすことは難しいことですが、効果的なイディオムを使うことで、より英語がはずむこともまた事実です。80のレッスンで600以上のイディオムの使い方が自然に身につきます。へそくり(a nest egg)、言い訳(a song and dance)など日常生活でよく使われる表現が満載です。

8 マナー違反の英会話　英語にだって「敬語」があります

ジェームス・M・バーダマン、森本豊富 共著　　　208ページ　ISBN 4-7700-2520-3

英語にだって「敬語」はあります。文法的には何の誤りもない「正しい英語」表現ですが、"I want you to write a letter of recommendation." （推薦状を書いてくれ）なんてぶっきらぼうな英語で依頼されたら、教授だってムッとしてしまうでしょう。「アメリカ人はフランクで開放的」と言われますが、お互いを傷つけないよう非常に気配りをしています。逆に、親しい仲間うちで丁寧な英語表現ばかりを使っていては、打ち解けられません。英語にだってTPOがあります。場に応じた英語表現を使い分けましょう。

10 「英語モード」で英会話　これがネイティブの発想法

脇山怜、佐野キム・マリー 共著　　　　　　　　224ページ　ISBN 4-7700-2522-X

英語でコミュニケーションをするときには、日本語から英語へ、「モード」のスイッチを切り替えましょう。タテ社会の日本では、へりくだって相手を持ち上げることが、人間関係の処世術とされています。ところが、「未経験で何もわかりませんがよろしく」のつもりで "I am inexperienced and I don't know anything." なんて英語で言えば、それはマイナスの自己イメージを投影することになるでしょう。「日本語モード」の英語は誤解のもとです。

11 英語で読む「科学ニュース」　話題の知識を英語でGet!

松野守峰 著　　　　　　　　　　　　　　　　208ページ　ISBN 4-7700-2456-8

科学に関する知識とことばが同時に身につく、画期的な英語実用書。「ネット恐怖症族」「スマート・マウスパッド」から「デザイナー・ドラッグ」「DNAによる全人類の祖先解明」まで、いま話題の科学情報が英語でスラスラ読めるようになります。ていねいな語句解説と豊富な用語リストにより、ボキャブラリーも大幅アップ！

12-1 CDブック 英会話・ぜったい・音読　[入門編]　英語の基礎回路を作る本

國弘正雄 編　久保野雅史 トレーニング指導　千田潤一 レッスン選択
　　　　　　　　　　　　　　　　　160ページ CD (25分)付　ISBN 4-7700-2746-X

「勉強」するだけでは、使える英語は身につきません。スポーツと同じで「練習」が必要です。使える英語を身につけるには、読んで内容がわかる英文を、自分の身体が覚え込むまで、繰り返し声を出して読んでみることです。音読、そして筆写という、いわば英語の筋肉トレーニングを自分自身でやってみて、初めて英語の基礎回路が自分のなかに構築出来るのです。中学1、2生用の英語教科書から選び抜いた12レッスンで、「読める英語」を「使える英語」に変えてしまいましょう。まずは3カ月、だまされたと思って練習してみると、確かな身体の変化にきっと驚くことでしょう。

12-2 CDブック 英会話・ぜったい・音読　頭の中に英語回路を作る本

國弘正雄 編　千田潤一 トレーニング指導　144ページ CD (40分)付　ISBN 4-7700-2459-2

英語を身につけるには、英語の基礎回路を作ることが先決です。家を建てる際、基礎工事をすることなしに、柱を立てたり、屋根を作るなんてことはしないはずです。英語もこれと同じです。基礎回路が出来ていない段階で、雑多な新しい知識を吸収しようとしても、ざるで水をすくうようなものです。単語や構文などをいくら覚えたとしても、実際の場面では自由には使えません。英語を身体で覚える…、それには、何と言っても音読です。本書には、中学3年生用の文部省認定済み英語教科書7冊から、成人の英語トレーニングに適した12レッスンを厳選して収録しました。だまされたと思って、まずは3ヵ月続けてみてください。確かな身体の変化にきっと驚かれることでしょう。

12-3 CDブック 英会話・ぜったい・音読　[挑戦編]　英語の上級回路を作る本

國弘正雄 編　千田潤一 トレーニング指導　160ページ CD (45分)付　ISBN 4-7700-2784-2

「使える英語」を身につけるには、徹底的に足腰を鍛える必要があります。「分かる」と「使える」は大違いです。「分かる」だけでは使える英語はぜったいに身につきません。「分かる英語」を「使える英語」にするには、スポーツと同じで、「練習」が欠かせません。そのためには、何と言っても音読です。日常会話はできるけど、交渉や説得はなかなか…、そんな方のため、高校1年生用の文部省検定済み英語教科書から10レッスンを厳選しました。まずは3カ月、本書でトレーニングしてみると、確かな身体の変化にきっと驚かれることでしょう。

15-1 AorB？ ネイティブ英語　日本人の勘違い150パターン

ジェームス・M・バーダマン 著　　　　　　　192ページ　ISBN 4-7700-2708-7

日本人英語には共通の「アキレス腱」があります。アメリカ人の筆者が、身近でもっとも頻繁に見聞きする、日本人英語の間違い・勘違いを約150例、一挙にまとめて解説しました。間違いを指摘し、背景を解説するだけでなく、実践的な例文、関連表現も盛り込みましたので、日本人共通の弱点を克服できます。これらの150パターンさえ気をつければ、あなたの英語がグンと通じるようになることでしょう。

15-2 AorB？ネイティブ英語II　どっちが正しい、この英語？

ジェームス・M・バーダマン 著　　192ページ　　ISBN 4-7700-2921-7

初心者・上級者にかかわらず、日本人英語には特有の間違いがあります。第I巻に引き続き、そんな日本人英語特有の間違い例を、さらに140パターン紹介しました。間違いを紹介するだけでなく、その間違いや勘違いがどうして生じたのかを、ネイティブの観点から、日本人向けに解説してあります。これら日本人共通の弱点を克服すれば、英語の間違いを格段に減らすことができます。

16　英語でEメールを書く　ビジネス＆パーソナル「世界基準」の文例集

田中宏昌、ブライアン・アズビョンソン 共著　　224ページ　　ISBN 4-7700-2566-1

Eメールはこんなに便利。英文Eメールは、他の英文ライティングとどう違う？　気を付けなければならないポイントは？　など、Eメールのマナーからビジネスでの使いこなし方、さらには個人的な仲間の増やし方やショッピングの仕方まで、様々な場面で使える実例を豊富に掲載しました。例文には考え方をも解説してありますので、応用が簡単に出来ます。また英文には対訳が付いています。

19　CDブック 英会話・つなぎの一言　質問すれば会話がはずむ！

浦島 久、クライド・ダブンポート 共著　　240ページ CD（62分）付　　ISBN 4-7700-2728-1

質問は相手の答えを聞き取るための最大のヒント！　初級者（TOEIC350～530点　英検3級～準2級）向けの質問例文集。英会話にチャレンジしたものの、相手の英語がまったく理解できなかった、あるいは、会話がつながらなかった、という経験はありませんか？　そんなときは、積極的に質問してみましょう。自分の質問に対する相手の答えは理解できるはずです。つまり、質問さえできれば相手の英語はある程度わかるようになるのです。ドンドン質問すれば、会話もつながり、それはまた、リスニング強化にもつながります。本書では、質問しやすい99のテーマに1800の質問文例を用意しました。

20　似ていて違う英単語　コリンズコービルド英語表現使い分け辞典

エドウィン・カーペンター 著　斎藤早苗 訳　　256ページ　　ISBN 4-7700-2484-3

SayとTellはどう違う？　最新の生きている英語　使い分け辞典　英語には英和辞書を引いても、違いがわからない単語がいくつもあります。そんな一見同じに見える表現にはどんな違いがあるのだろうか。どう使い分けると良いのだろう。そんな疑問に答えるのが本書です。Collins COBUILDの誇る3億語以上の英語のデータベースの分析から生まれた辞典です。例文も豊富に掲載しました。

22　チャートでわかるaとanとthe　ネイティブが作った冠詞ナビ

アラン・ブレンダー 著　　288ページ　　ISBN 4-7700-2643-9

最も基本的でありながら最も理解されていない単語aとanとthe。冠詞は最も頻繁に使われる英単語トップ10にランクされ、日本人が決してスペリングの間違いをしない単語でありながら、日本人の中で正確に理解している人がほとんどいないという不思議な単語です。本書では、冠詞の機能を単独にではなく、主語や動詞との一致、語順、文脈、話者の心理などから多面的に説明することで十分な理解と応用力が得られるよう工夫しています。

24　こんな英語がわからない！？　日本人が知らないネイティブの日常フレーズ386

ジェームス・M・バーダマン 著　岸本幸枝 編訳　　272ページ　　ISBN 4-7700-2830-X

とっても簡単な単語、数語の組み合わせなのに、どんな意味かわからない。ネイティブの日常会話では、こんなフレーズが飛び交います。難しい単語を覚える前に、実際に使われるこれらの表現の補強をしましょう。本書では、教科書やテキストだけでは知ることのできない日常的なフレーズの中から、とくに日本人の盲点となっているものを厳選して、詳しい解説と会話例をつけて紹介しました。これがわかれば気分はネイティブです。

25　英語で電話をかける　これだけは必要これだけで十分

ブライアン・アズビョンソン、田中宏昌 共著　　224ページ　　ISBN 4-7700-2835-0

言葉だけで意志を伝えるのは難しい。それが英語ならなおさらです。電話でのコミュニケーションが難しいのは、表情などが伝わらないからです。しかし、電話の会話にもそれなりのコミュニケーションのストラテジーがあるのです。それさえ理解すれば、それほど苦労せずに電話を使いこなすことができます。効果的なフレーズが豊富に掲載されていますので、ビジネスにプライベートに、様々な場面ですぐに活用ができます。

27 謎の英単語230　日本人にはわからない「裏」の意味

ボイエ・デ・メンテ、松本道弘 共著　　　　　　256ページ　ISBN 4-7700-2883-0

一見とても簡単そうなのに、どうにも意味がわからない、そんな単語や熟語が、現代英語にはたくさんあります。それがLoaded English (多彩な意味をもつ、含みのある英語)です。これらは、欧米の英語では日常的に使われているものの、日本にはない文化や発想のために、たいていの日本人には理解しづらいのです。この本は、そうしたパワフルで、人気が高く、そして味のある、230のLoaded Englishを厳選し、その背景と本当の意味と、実際の使われ方を説明してあります。現代英語のキーワードが使いこなせるようになる本書は、英文雑誌や英字紙や、さまざまなペーパーバックを読む上でも不可欠のものです。

28 CDブック「プロ英語」入門　通訳者が実践している英語練習法

鳥飼玖美子 著　　　　　　176ページ CD (23分)付　ISBN 4-7700-2836-9

「シャドーイング」「サイト・トランスレーション」「ボキャビル」……。本書では、通訳者養成課程で採り入れられている訓練方法の中から、一般の英語学習者が応用できる練習方法を、レッスン付きでご紹介します。「ビジネスで使える英語を身につけたい」「ボランティア通訳くらいは出来るようになりたい」……。それなら、自分の習熟度や目的を考慮しながら、プロがすすめるこんな方法で練習してみませんか。今まで苦手だった「長文読解」「リスニング」「要約」なども、この方法なら克服できることでしょう。

29 「英語モード」でライティング　ネイティブ式発想で英語を書く

大井恭子 著　　　　　　192ページ　ISBN 4-7700-2834-2

「英語で書く」時には、英語式発想の書き方をすることです。日本人の書いた英語の文章は、「文法的には正しいが、何を言いたいのかがさっぱり分からない！」としばしば指摘されます。文法的に正しいことは、もちろん望ましいことですが、英語で書く時には英語式考え方で書かなければ、せっかく書いた企画書やレポートも読んでもらえません。英語を書くためには、「英語式書き方」の基本をまず身につけましょう。「英語で書く」を通じて、英語式発想の方法を身につけたら、英会話やプレゼンテーションだって、後はその応用です。

30 ビジネスに出る英単語　テーマ別重要度順キーワード2500

松野守峰、松林博文、鶴岡公幸 共著　　　　　656ページ　ISBN 4-7700-2718-4

「実践ですぐに役立つ」、「知らないと致命的」、そんな最重要ビジネス英単語2500を厳選！本書の特徴●キーコンセプト(用語の基本概念)を徹底解説●最新キーワードを含む2500語を分野別・重要度順に配列●同義語・反義語・関連語・頻出イディオムを併記●現場に密着した"生きた"表現を学べる用例を豊富に収録●MBA取得、TOEIC対策に最適

31 語源で覚える最頻出イディオム　意味がわかればこんなにカンタン！

マーヴィン・ターバン 著　松野守峰、宮原知子 共訳　　352ページ　ISBN 4-7700-2723-0

英語を聞いたり読んだりしていると日常的に出てくる600以上の最頻出イディオムの意味と由来についてわかりやすく解説！イディオムがややこしいのは、イディオムの意味と、そのイディオムを構成する1つ1つの単語の意味がほとんど関係ないからです。でも、その由来がわかれば頭にスラスラ入ってきます。例えば、"let the cat out of the bag"は「秘密を漏らす」という意味です。今では、このイディオムはcat「猫」やbag「袋」と何ら関係がありませんが、何百年もの昔には関係がありました。猫を袋に入れて豚だと偽って高く売ろうとしたら猫が出てきてしまったことに由来しているからです。どうですか？イディオムの隠された由来がわかれば、覚えるのに便利でしょ?!

32 ダメ！その英語 [日常生活編]　暮らしの英語NG集

連東孝子 著　　　　　　192ページ　ISBN 4-7700-2922-5

帰宅した同僚あての電話を受けて、"He left the company." と言ったら、「えっ、彼は退職したの！」と相手を驚かせてしまった立野さん……。日本人が「誤解した例」、「誤解された例」、「日々の生活と交流の中で気持ちがうまく伝わらなかった例」を、アメリカ滞在歴30余年になる著者が、約110のエピソードを通してご紹介します。アメリカ生活を疑似体験しながら、日本人英語のウイークポイントが克服できます。

あなたの英語が変わる **TOEIC対策に最適！**

講談社パワー・イングリッシュ

ホームページ　http://www.kodansha-intl.co.jp

（CDブック）
英会話・ぜったい・音読

頭の中に英語回路を作る本

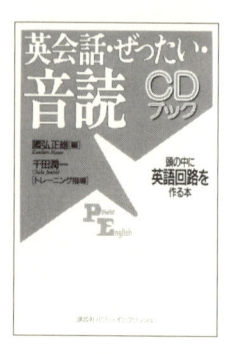

「勉強」するだけでは、使える英語は身につきません。スポーツと同じで「練習」が必要です。使える英語を身につけるには、読んで内容がわかる英文を、自分の身体が覚え込むまで、繰り返し声を出して読んでみることです。音読、そして筆写という、いわば英語の筋肉トレーニングを自分自身でやってみて、初めて英語の基礎回路が自分のなかに構築出来るのです。

"聴く・話す・読む・書く"の4機能をフル活用し、「読める英語」を「使える英語」に変えてしまいましょう。まずは3カ月、だまされたと思って練習してみると、確かな身体の変化にきっと驚くことでしょう。

中学3年生用の英語教科書から12レッスンを厳選して収録しました。
國弘正雄　千田潤一 トレーニング指導　144ページ CD (40分)付　ISBN 4-7700-2459-2

CDブック **英会話・ぜったい・音読** [入門編]　英語の基礎回路を作る本

中学1、2年生用の英語教科書から選び抜いた12レッスン。
國弘正雄　久保野雅史 トレーニング指導　千田潤一 レッスン選択
160ページ CD (25分)付　ISBN 4-7700-2746-X

CDブック **英会話・ぜったい・音読** [挑戦編]　英語の上級回路を作る本

高校1年生用の英語教科書から選び抜いた10レッスン。
國弘正雄 編　千田潤一 トレーニング指導　160ページ CD (45分)付　ISBN 4-7700-2784-2

TOEICスコアの目安

400点	500点	600点	700点	800点
英会話・ぜったい・音読 [入門編]				
		英会話・ぜったい・音読		
			英会話・ぜったい・音読 [挑戦編]	

ビジネスに出る英単語

テーマ別重要度順 キーワード2500

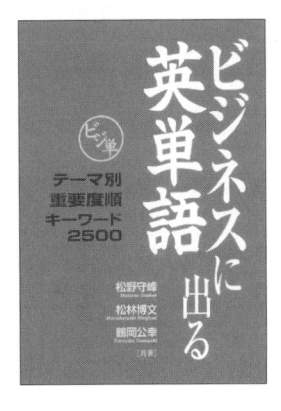

"生き残る"ビジネスマンのための英単語集

ビジ単。™

松野守峰、松林博文、鶴岡公幸 [共著]

四六判変型　仮製　656ページ
ISBN 4-7700-2718-4

- MBAと実務経験をあわせ持つ著者が収録語彙を厳選
- ジャンル別(マーケティング、生産管理、財務・経理など)に分類、重要度順に配列
- 見出し語：2,500/総収録語彙：10,000(類義語・反義語・派生語等含む)
- 訳語を提示するのみならず、日本語の語彙そのものを平明な表現で十分に解説
- 解説部分では国名・都市名・企業名を具体的に挙げ、ビジネス界のナマ情報を提供
- 辞書的な解釈では誤訳となりやすい語は、ビジネス的見地から特に解説・用例を付記
- 米語・英語間の定義の差異を明示
- 重要略語は見出し語として採用
- 検索が容易な英和&和英インデックスつき
- 見やすく、暗記にも便利な2色刷り

TOEIC® Test 「正解」が見える

読むだけで50点、練習すれば200点UP
（著者談）

キム・デギュン 著
樋口謙一郎 訳

A5判 仮製 336頁 CD1枚(60分)つき
ISBN 4-7700-2961-6

韓国のTOEICスコアは、なぜ日本より高いのか。

世界最多!? 60回以上TOEICを受験し続けた男が解明した「出題と正答のメカニズム」。韓国で85万人の読者を獲得した"対策の切り札"が、ついに日本上陸!

第1部
各パート(I〜VII)別に問題形式と正答する秘訣を伝授
▼
はじめて受験する方にも、再受験者にもおすすめ!

第2部
文法、語法問題の「急所」を征服
▼
文法・語法にも完全対応!

第3部
TOEIC必出の最重要単語を習得
▼
CDでボキャビル

これ1冊でOK!